The Overkilling the Past trilogy is available now

BOOK 1

Overkilling the Past

BOOK 2

WHAT COMES AROUND The Story of Karma

BOOK 3

Detective Lucas: End of an Error

Detective Lucas: End of an Error

Copyright ©□ 2025

William L. Ash

ISBN: 979-8-9926441-3-5

Printed in the United States * Irving, Texas 75038

Ashfam Publishing

Contact: Leeash35@yahoo.com

This one is for me.

"Oh, you're awake. Welcome back to the land of the living, my dear. I've been taking care of you for the last 3 days. How are you feeling?" A smiling nurse asked.

"Thirsty," Karma said through a dry throat. Her entire body hurt. "What happened? I feel like I been hit by a truck."

"You were. Several, actually," the nurse replied.

Karma's memory came back in a flash.

"Wait! My friend. Patricia. Is she ok? Where is she?" Karma tried to sit up but was held down by a back brace she couldn't see. Her body was heavily bandaged. Her right leg was in a cast. "There were other people in my car!" she said excitedly.

"As far as I know, you were the only one in that wreck. You're lucky to be alive," the nurse said, continuing to do her job, checking the monitors and filling out her charts. "Do you need anything? I'm going to have the doctor come in and check on you. Here's the TV remote and your phone. Press the red button if you need anything," the nurse said soothingly, before leaving.

Karma was confused. 'What happened to…?'

"Oh. I forgot. Someone left this for you." The nurse came back in and handed her an overfilled, yellow shipping envelope.

Opening it immediately, Karma reached in and grabbed a Peppermint Pattie candy bar. Looking inside, she pulled out three figurines: a Wonder Woman, a Captain Marvel, and a Princess Leia, the same ones that she saw on Celeste's desk. There was a small tag on Wonder Woman's foot with the letters DC.

"You bitch," Karma whispered, smiling to herself.

The next item she pulled out was an Avenger's postcard that read, "Yes, I forgive you. Will you forgive me?"

"Of course," Karma cried, wiping her eyes. Finally, after taking a deep breath, she pulled out an old school iPod and its headphones. A sticky note attached said, Press play.

She was an emotional wreck by the time she put them over her ears, and there was no amount of tissues that would stop the flow of tears as Sister Sledge sang the chorus to their 1979 hit, "We are family. I got all my sisters and me."

DETECTIVE LUCAS

END OF AN ERROR

WILLIAM L. ASH

I ain't a killer but don't push me / revenge is like the sweetest joy next to getting pussy – 2Pac

Prelude to the intro

I used to think people were good. I remember how I used to think that even though people had different backgrounds, we were all the same. Sure, we've all made questionable decisions, but everyone was still generally good.

Maybe I was naïve, but I had always figured that everyone wanted the same basic things: love, peace, and happiness. We all just wanted to raise our kids, be good neighbors, smile, laugh, and have fun with our friends.

Remember that old story about the lady who steals bread to feed her starving kids? That woman wasn't a bad person; her choice wasn't the best, but that didn't make her 'bad'.

Like religion. At its core, all religions are basically the same. Be honest, be charitable, love thy neighbor, help when you can, do the right thing.

I used to believe that bad people were just misguided people, and if given the right tools, they would see the light and change.

Well, I was wrong.

Some people really are just bad. Some people just come out of the womb evil. It's crazy to think that there are actually human beings who feel good when they see others suffer. There are people who thrive on despair and sadness, and are so selfish that they don't care how their actions affect anyone else. They torture helpless animals. They set fire to people's property. They inflict as much hurt and pain on innocent people as they can. They do bad just for the sake of doing bad.

And I know they know better. Everyone knows right from wrong, some people just choose wrong over right.

It took me a while to realize this, but once I did, it hit me like a ton of bricks. I remember feeling betrayed, like I'd been lied to. It was like learning that Santa Claus wasn't real, or that magicians weren't really magic, or that your dad wasn't your real dad...

But I digress.

As I sat on a bus headed upstate, every so often, I caught my reflection in the window. I saw the tired eyes of a man who's seen too much tragedy. I saw laugh lines etched in the skin of a man who's cried too many tears. I saw the look of determination on the face of a man who, through it all, has kept his promise to serve and protect those who can't protect themselves.

Hello, I'm Detective Dewayne Lucas. I'm the good guy.

Chapter 1: Shit happens

I was born in a small town on the East Coast, about 30 miles west of Boston, Massachusetts. I was raised mostly by my grandparents because my mom was a worthless crack addict who was more interested in taking drugs than taking care of me. And nobody knows who my dad was. It could've been anyone. There were so many different men in and out of my life in the early days, it didn't even matter.

She stayed high during her pregnancy, and I was born premature and addicted to heroin, which is exactly why I'm so short now.

My size used to bother me; I was teased relentlessly my whole life. I've been called Webster. Mini me. Arnold, from that one show with the 'Whatchu talking bout Willis?' I've heard it all, and if I'm being honest, some of them were kind of funny. I mean, when someone said they felt bad because they knew I'd never reach my goals, I actually did laugh. Or the joke about the grass tickling my balls when I ran across a field... That was pretty funny, too.

In school, there was this guy who would call me something different every day of the week. Sleepy, Sneezy, Grumpy... Ha, ha, even my teachers jumped on that one. I couldn't have a girlfriend unless she could deal with everyone calling her Snow White.

In hindsight, I know they were just jokes, kids are mean. I'm 5'3" now, and I'm an adult, but as a kid, I didn't know how to handle my emotions. I fought a lot, and got my ass beat. A lot.

I remember going home crying, only to get pushed right back out the door by a grandmother who wouldn't allow me to be no, 'punk ass bitch!' My grandfather was a pastor, and always at the church, so I didn't have anyone to protect me. I had to fight.

I'm grateful for those days because I learned how to defend myself both mentally and physically. I learned to just shake it off (Mariah, not Taylor) and stop letting the little things bother me so much. It made me the person I am today.

I had an older brother who I didn't know about until I was a teenager. I'd idolized him since the first day we met. He was the coolest guy everywhere we went. He was tall, good-looking, and a good athlete. He had all the girls. He didn't take shit from anyone, and wouldn't let anybody make fun of me. He was my hero, he could do no wrong in my eyes. I absolutely worshipped my brother Antonio… T-Bone.

It was his death that made me want to become a detective. I remember it like it was yesterday.

T-Bone had gone off to college. He had a full athletic scholarship to the school he'd always wanted to go to. He was living his dream. We talked every day. He'd tell me about all the parties, his coaches, his classes… Everything. He knew how bad I wanted to go, and he made sure to make me feel like I was there. He told me how, after class, him and a group of friends would go to a local bar to drink and hang out.

He told me about how much college was like high school when it came to the social hierarchy. There were the jocks, who were at the top, then the hot girls who were there for the jocks. Then the fans, who were basically anonymous, and then the nerds. Below them were the folks he called the jesters. These were the people who would do anything to fit in. They were just there for all the other group's entertainment. They were the ones who laughed the loudest, even when they were being made fun of. They paid for the drinks, even though they were often not part of any toasts. They were the designated drivers, even though they were never invited to any of the parties they drove the cool kids to.

He told me about one particular jester he nicknamed Charlie Brown. He talked about how wild Charlie was, and how he liked the guy, but warned me to watch out for people like him. Charlie Brown acted on emotion. He was impulsive, overzealous, and lived like he had no original thoughts. He just did anything anyone said, with no care for his own well-being. T-Bone told me that people who didn't care for themselves could never be trusted. I carried that advice with me my whole life.

Me and my brother's calls went on for his entire freshman year, then suddenly, on the third day into his sophomore year, they stopped.

A day passed, but I knew he had a big game coming up, and he wasn't doing so well with his playbook, so I figured he was busy. I was a senior in high school, finally had a girlfriend, and was feeling good about life. I had my own distractions, one missed call wasn't a big deal.

Until it was.

When my grandmother walked into my room that day, I already had my phone in my hand. I had just started dialing my brothers fucking number!

T-Bone had been murdered. He'd been found dead in the front seat of his beloved Trans Am, Kitt. When I got to the station, they said he'd been nearly decapitated. They said his head was only held on by a tendon.

I had never dealt with death before. I'd never even had a goldfish die on me. I had no life lessons to help me cope with all the stuff I had going on inside my head. I will never forget the callousness and the dismissiveness of the officer handling the case. I hated everything about him.

The way he shrugged his shoulders when he pushed my brother's murder scene pictures across the table at me. The way he kept getting up to refill his coffee cup, then stood around the coffee machine, laughing and joking with his coworkers. The way he dismissed all of my questions with a, 'Shit happens, kid,' so nonchalantly, as if this type of thing happened every day.

The final straw was weeks later when I went to check in on the progress of the case. He looked me in my face and said, "Look, kid. There are no leads. We have nothing. We're probably not going to find the killer. Honestly, with a case like this, my captain will probably just call it a suicide. We have to close cases, ya know? It limits the paperwork. I'm sorry about your brother, but shit happens."

I was hurt, angry, and frustrated. I felt disrespected. I felt that they disrespected my brother. I wanted to kill the detective. I felt so helpless, and back then, there were no hashtags where I could go online and rally for support. There were no such things as defund the police (which is a horrible idea by the way). I just had to accept it. There was nothing I could do. That's when I decided what my career path would be. That was the only way I could prevent this from happening to anyone else. I wanted to be that bridge between the crime and the victim. Nobody should be victimized twice. Grieving people deserved more than, 'Shit happens.'

"Hey! Do I know you from somewhere?" A voice woke me up out of my memory.

"What? No," I replied, irritated at being bothered.

"Yeah, I know you. You look like that little cop, detective guy. You look like the asshole that busted my uncle!"

I finally looked over at the person interrupting my thoughts. A large man with a giant swastika tattooed on his face stared down at me from a seat across the aisle.

"Nope, wasn't me," I said flatly, looking away. I wasn't worried, I knew his type, all mouth. He's used to being bigger and louder than everyone else, so he used that intimidation to bully people, but when it came down to it, though he sat on this bus a prisoner like me, headed to court, his crimes were not violent. Drugs, breaking and entering, maybe, but not violence. One look at his unscarred, normal-looking hands confirmed that. He wasn't a fighter.

"He's dead, you know? It's your fault. You busted him, he went to jail and those assholes murdered him! IT'S YOUR FUCKING FAULT!"

I had no idea who this guy's uncle was, and I really didn't care. We were both handcuffed and shackled, along with the other 12 guys on the bus, on our way to see Judge Hutchinson, who would probably release all of us with our own form of light sentences, probation, or community service. We weren't hardened criminals, we were being moved from holding cells to the court.

I wasn't afraid of that guy, even as he continued to yell, "YOU KILLED MY FAVORITE UNCLE!" and worked himself into a frenzy..

I turned back to look at him. "Hey, I'm sorry about your uncle, but shit happens."

Chapter 2: Lost control

I wasn't too worried as I walked into the courtroom. I've crossed paths with this judge many times over the years. In my mind, this was an open-and-shut case. It was just a formality.

"Mr. Lucas, not *detective* anymore?" the judge asked.

"Not officially, sir, no. I'm just consulting now," I replied respectfully.

"But it says here that you identified yourself as a detective when you apprehended the suspect."

"Old habits die hard, sir. It was a crime in progress, I did what came natural in the moment. I said the wrong words, and it shouldn't have happened. My apologies." I spoke confidently. I'd been on both sides of many courtrooms many times. I knew the game.

I'd gone from a regular street officer to detective, to detective on a TV show (which was a bad mistake). I went from that to working as a private investigator, then on to what I do now, consulting. I was hired to this district to help with a string of high-profile murders.

The reason I was standing in front of Judge Hutchinson now started innocently enough. I was simply following up on a person of interest, who happened to work in an office building downtown. As I walked down the hallway, I heard the unmistakable sounds of struggle. A trained ear can hear these things. It wasn't the normal sound that you'd hear in an office building, so I opened a door where I thought it came from and saw a man standing over a young woman.

Both were fully dressed, and neither had any physical signs of distress, but I knew what was happening. I've seen a lot of bad things, and even though her mouth didn't say she needed help, her eyes did. I jumped at the larger man immediately, taking him down with two quick punches to the midsection. As he doubled over, I threw an uppercut that broke the mandible in his jaw, destroying his face, as blood shot from both his mouth and nose simultaneously. His body made the sound of defeat. It was the sound of a giant balloon losing all of its air at once. I moved behind him and twisted his arms behind his back, which pulled his shoulders together. I squeezed until the clavicle went 'pop', then his body went limp.

"I am Detective Lucas and you are under arrest, goddamnit!" I growled angrily.

Admittedly, I'd lost control. But there was something about the look in the young woman's eyes. It was a look I'd seen before. It was the look of someone who was horrified at first, then relieved when she saw me and recognized she'd been saved. It was the look that said everything would be alright.

It was the same look that my estranged daughter, Karma, had for me so many years ago, and where there, I failed, here, I did not.

It turned out that the guy was a lawyer and the son of some politician. A known asshole and womanizer. I was arrested the next day, but wasn't charged with assault. Apparently, the dad knew his son needed his ass kicked.

Judge Hutchinson removed his glasses and spoke firmly, "I know you're well aware that the charge of impersonating an officer can get you up to 10 years in prison, but I know you. I know what you did and why you did it. You've served your community well for years, and I'm going to let you go with a warning and a bit of advice. Reapply for your badge, DETECTIVE Lucas. We can use more good men like you. CASE DISMISSED. NEXT!"

I nodded at the judge as an officer removed my cuffs, then turned to walk out, but not before blowing a kiss at swastika face as I passed by.

I went to 7-11 for a 6 pack of 2 X's (as I like to call them) and drove my pickup to my honey hole by the lake. My trusty fishing pole is a permanent fixture in the backseat, and throughout the years, this has always been my relief. In all of my travels around the country, the first thing I do is find a quiet place where I can put a line in the water.

It gives me a chance to not think. I'm able to untangle the rats nest of thoughts that seem to clog up my brain during the course of a regular day. I've probably solved more cases near a body of water than anywhere else. It's like the sound of the water, and the peace that it brings me, unlocks a stream of consciousness that I'm not able to tap into without it. I've heard musicians say that they don't create songs. They say the music is already there, they just have to reach out and grab it.

I always thought it was funny when I was called a great detective. I have a reputation for seeing things others miss. I've even heard people half jokingly wonder if I was an accomplice on some of the cases I've solved. But no, sometimes I just drop a line in the lake and the cases solve themselves.

'Reapply for detective, huh?' I thought, as I looked across the lake at a woman and her two small children digging in the dirt on the shore. They reminded me of my own…

Beep Beep Beep

"FUCK!" I yelled. "Damn phone!" I forgot to shut off the ringer.

"Hello?" I answered reluctantly. I got a bite on the line as soon as the district's Lieutenant started talking.

"Damnit!" I dropped my phone, spilled my beer in my lap, and knocked over my tackle box all at the same time. "Hold on," I yelled, hoping he heard me.

I tucked my phone into my shoulder as I reeled in a small bass that I quickly released.

He told me that there was another murder not far from where I was. I packed up my stuff and drove to the crime scene.

A uniformed officer met me at a toll gate on the edge of a bridge that crossed a major river. He escorted me to where the body was laid out under a blue tarp, just like you see in the movies. A rope ran from underneath it and was tied to the railing of the bridge.

"Be careful, detective, this isn't normal," the officer said.

I waved my hand dismissively, annoyed at the chaotic crime scene. Whoever was supposed to be in charge had lost control. "Let's see it," I said.

He pulled back the tarp slowly, starting at the feet. The male victim's legs were mangled, bent, and twisted in different directions as if he'd been hit by a truck. The torso was exposed, cut open with the intestines hanging out. One of the victim's hands was in the same shape as his legs, the other was missing the middle finger.

I saw the rope was still around his neck, which added to my irritation. I looked up at the officer and shook my head, annoyed.

The victim's expression still wore the look of horror he must've felt as the killer stuffed the middle finger in his mouth. He'd been severely beaten, and the bumps and bruises disfigured the shape of his head. He would've been unrecognizable if it wasn't for the giant swastika tattoo on his face.

Chapter 3: Lieutenant Dan, ice cream

"I'm getting too old for this shit," I said, standing, using the old Lethal Weapon line. I looked around the briefing room at the other detectives, who all wore the same expression.

There were no leads. There was nothing that linked the murders together. There were no persons of interest. The only similarities I could see that nobody mentioned were the brutality of the murders.

"Any thoughts?" Lieutenant Dan walked up to me with his hand extended, looking as lost as everyone else.

I accepted his greeting and shook my head no, then said, "These seem personal, don't they? This guy ain't just killing, he's butchering them. Almost like he's trying to make a point."

"I got forensics looking for any kind of connections between the victims now," he replied. He carried an impatient air about him.

"Whoever it was had to be strong. Swastika face is a big dude to just be able to lift up and over that railing. And in broad daylight? He would've had to move quick," I said.

"Or, maybe he had someone help him?" Lieutenant Dan offered.

I hadn't thought of that. At this point, everything was a possibility. Hell, he could be the killer for all I knew. It wasn't him, though.

I've known Lieutenant Dan for a long time. He's the good guy. He's the guy you want on your team. He's the guy you want showing up when your mom or your daughter calls 911. He treats every victim with the same respect he asks for himself. He treats every case as if he were the person who lost a loved one. He, like me, has been that person before. I remember the day we met.

I was still just the guy from the popular 48 Hours TV show back then, and I was assigned to a case that never made it to screen. A popular youth coach had been brutally murdered on the side of the road. The guy was a pillar in the community, donating his time to troubled youth, coaching and mentoring kids of all backgrounds, fighting the good fight.

By the time I showed up, the vehicle that had crushed the man's sternum had already been lifted and stood on jack stands, minus a tire. It looked like he'd attempted to fix a flat, and the car fell on him. Horrible, but not uncommon. I was irritated that I was called to deal with this, yelling at whoever

*could hear me, 'I AM A GODDAMNED DETECTIVE, NOT A
FUCKING CORONER!' (Yes, I was an arrogant SOB back
then.)*

*As I walked away, back towards my car, I heard a yell. A
primal scream that stopped everyone who heard it in their
tracks.*

*Daniel Nash, not a lieutenant back then, had just arrived and
saw his brother dead on the street. I went back to the scene,
which was becoming chaotic, and saw what I had never
bothered to look at before. The man on the ground wasn't just
crushed, he'd been stabbed. Repeatedly. Disgustingly. His
upper torso was a mangled mess of flesh and bone. A pair of
what looked like blue, latex gloves were left sticking out of
what should've been the man's belly button. I turned my head
and threw up on the sidewalk.*

*Me and Daniel Nash bonded over the fact that we'd both lost
someone we loved to a senseless act of violence.*

*We became friends as we tried to solve his brother's murder,
only for it to become another unsolved mystery. Another cold
case.*

I felt goosebumps thinking about that night.

I struggled with the urge not to say my old long-running joke
I had for him.

I said it anyway, hoping to lighten the mood, and maybe reset
our brains. "Hey. Lieutenant Dan. Maybe he killed him, then

had to run to the forest… Get it? He ran to the forest… to get some ice cream… Lieutenant Dan, ice cream… No?" I said the last part just like Tom Hanks did in the movie.

"Hardy har," my friend replied with a reluctant smile.

Since the joke didn't land, I went back to being serious.

"That kind of brutality. It kinda reminds me of, I mean, I ain't seen something that bad since…" I didn't finish. I didn't need to state the obvious.

"Yeah, I know," he said, sadly.

The lieutenant patted me on the shoulder and walked away, shaking his head.

I sat there thinking, going over the basics in my mind, making sure I didn't skip any steps. A typical murder can happen for any reason. It can be an argument over a parking spot or in traffic, which might end with one or two gunshots. It could be a robbery where someone gets killed. In a mass shooting, victims are usually hit once or twice before the killer moves on. Even a stabbing at a bar, on the street… Those are usually one or two wounds, maybe more, but it's very rarely a repeated, continuous action.

Crimes of passion are different. They are personal. This is where you see multiple stab wounds. Multiple gunshots. It's as if the person doing the killing is in such a rage that one wound isn't enough. Their anger is not satisfied until they get it all out.

That's how this felt. Whoever did this hated swastika face. The guy was an asshole, there was a lot to hate, but this just felt different for some reason.

This guy was already dead by the time he was hung over the bridge. Just like Lieutenant Dan's brother was already killed by the car smashing his rib cage, he didn't need to be stabbed too. Just like T-Bone was already…

Beep Beep Beep A text.

'Happy birthday, Daddy!'

Shit, was that today?

Chapter 4: Keisha and Karma

I do truly love my daughter Karma. You wouldn't know it by my actions. I've never done anything that would earn me a world's greatest dad mug. Or a father of the year trophy. I'd never been the support system every child needs and deserves. I could say I just did to her what my dad did to me, and leave it at that. I could blame it on the cycle of life. That's how I learned, so that's all I knew, but that's a bullshit excuse. Matter of fact, anyone who says that is full of shit. My situation was different, still one hundred percent my fault, but it was still different.

Here, I'm the bad guy.

I live with an unrelenting, unbearable, almost unmanageable amount of guilt when it comes to her. The thought of her brings up feelings of worthlessness. The Scarface quote where Tony Montana says, "All I have in this world is my balls and my word," is the defining term for every man. Every single adult male has code built into their DNA that says that this statement is true.

And I failed at both. I failed the two people that I'd sworn to care for and protect when they needed me the most. I am an absolute failure of a man. The thought of that day when my wife Keisha, Karma's mother, was killed is like a snuff film that plays in my mind over and over on a loop.

I was working a case at around the same time as the Lieutenant's brother's murder, which led me to a suspect. The case was essentially done. I had all the evidence I needed, but just wanted one more piece to make it a slam dunk in court. And I got it!

I was ready to make the arrest when the suspect kidnapped my family, Keisha and Karma, then threatened to shoot them both in the head if I didn't meet up with him immediately.

I hurried to a wooded area high above a lake on the edge of a cliff and saw Jhonny, the suspect, pointing a gun at my girls.

They were scared, but unharmed, and I had full confidence that I'd saved the day. Karma looked at me with the most grateful, loving, adoring, daddy's girl eyes.... Her hero had arrived, and everything was going to be ok.

All I had to do was use my negotiating skills and get him to let them go. He pleaded his case and begged me to believe that he was innocent. In hindsight, what he said made sense, but I couldn't see it then since he still had his gun pointed at their heads.

Out of nowhere, my best friend Charles Brown appeared, shot him in the head, then kicked him over the cliff and saved the day.

The whole scene was unbelievable! He was like some action hero from one of those ridiculous supermarket mini-novels that women seem to love.

In that moment, my friend Charles went from being a friend to being a brother.

Then it all changed. A call over my walkie-talkie from dispatch informed me that the forensic evidence about the murders that I'd requested had finally come in. Charles, the man who was now wrapped in the thankful embraces of my family, was the real killer.

I'd been tricked. I'd been hoodwinked, bamboozled. The suspect I had been chasing for the past couple of months had been standing beside me the whole time!

I looked over at him. He'd heard the radio call and knew he was caught, but before I could even get a word out, he turned his gun on Keisha and Karma.

I went into shock. There was no training for this. There were no protocols set in place for this type of thing. This was a plot twist I had no way of anticipating.

If this were one of those aforementioned novels, the writer would've deleted this whole chapter. It was unreal.

My mind was in chaos. Charles had one arm wrapped around Keisha's neck and held a violent handful of hair. His other hand held the gun that he had hit Karma on the head with. All while Keisha yelled obscenities at me to stop him.

*Then, **POP!***

Charles pulled the trigger, and my wife's head exploded.

In one moment, instinct took over, and I jumped at him. In the next, I was handcuffed to a tree, and my daughter was being dragged away through the woods. But then Charles stopped and came back.

He bent down and, in a whisper, told me about the time he tried to decapitate a college kid in the front seat of the guy's Trans-Am. He said the kid cried like a little baby.

I didn't yell as Charles dragged my daughter away into the woods. I didn't scream. I just stood there, a defeated man staring at my dead wife, replaying the last few minutes in my head, cursing myself for being a failure.

Charles Brown. He'd killed two people I loved, and just took off with another.

But even through all of that, it was the look in my daughter's eyes that hurt the worst. Such disappointment. There was so much shame and sadness in her eyes. Her hero was a fraud. Her hero was a weak, undersized man. Her hero was ordinary.

I decided then that when I got free, I would end it. There was no need for me to exist. I wish Charles would've just killed me, too. Head down, I started to cry.

"AAAAAAHH! MOMMY!"

Karma had come back up the hill by herself but was frozen in place at the sight of her mother's nearly headless body.

"BABY! LOOK AT ME!" I told her. "Look at me, love! HEY! Hey baby, look at me." I tried to speak calmly.

"Karma, baby, look at me. I need your help. I need you to help daddy, ok? Can you do that? Karma?"

She slowly turned to face me with tears in her eyes. She had a knot on her head from where that motherfucker hit her with his gun.

"There she is," I said, trying to sound cheerful, "Hey, come get the keys. Come get these keys out of my pocket and unlock daddy, ok? Can you do that, sweet girl?" I did my best to keep her focused on me. She nodded her head yes, then did as I asked.

"Sir? Excuse me, Mr. Lucas?" A voice asked, cautiously.

"Fuck. What damnit! What?" I was annoyed at being interrupted out of my memory.

An officer held out a vanilla ice cream cone, offering it to me. "The lieutenant said to give you this. Happy Birthday."

Chapter 5: Such a fucking baby

It had been 3 weeks since turning 50 when I got the call about another set of bodies being found. I was in the middle of a session with a psychiatrist about my depression, trying to talk through my issues, when the call came through.

Beep beep. Damn phone. I had forgotten to shut off the ringer again.

I drove to a construction site where two bodies were found in a dumpster, both crucified to the same makeshift cross made out of rebar. They were hung face to face, wrists and ankles bound together by fencing wire, with railroad stakes through the centers of their hands. For some reason, to me, it looked like some demented artists' vision of marriage. The two people, together forever, before a God that neither believes in.

I had officers pull them down to get a better look. Lieutenant Dan arrived shortly after, and I appreciated his presence as a trusted confidant, although active crime scenes were way below his rank.

The victims were separated and laid on their backs. The only thing in common between them was the matching kitchen knives sticking out of each of their chests. But that's where the similarities stopped. It almost looked like two different people did this.

The male's throat was ripped open and hollow. Except for the spine, there was nothing there. No muscle, no Adam's apple, no veins...

His hair had been burned off, but his face was surprisingly unaffected. It was as if the killer had intentionally wanted it to be recognized. The rest of the body, except his feet, which were burned worse than his head, looked unharmed.

Not so with the female.

The killer must have hated this woman. At first sight, she looked like she was 50lbs overweight, but after further inspection, you could see she was just bloated from being drowned and then pulled out of the water and hung here. She was missing an eye. Patches of her hair had been pulled violently from her head, and you could see bone underneath the torn away flesh. Her left cheek had been bruised, it was scarred, and the bone structure had collapsed. It looked as if the killer had hit her repeatedly with some type of small, blunt object. Her right cheek had a large bite mark.

The killer had cut out her tongue and shoved it in a broken bottle of vodka, which was stuffed in her pocket. Her fingernails had been removed on both hands, and the big toe on her left foot was missing. The killer, for whatever reason, hung a brand new visitor's name badge around the victim's neck on a lanyard that read, Hi, I'm Tyra.

I shook my head, stood, and was met by a knowing look from Lieutenant Dan, then walked back to my car.

This had Charles Brown written all over it. The brutality of these murders… To stab someone through the heart is one thing, but then to rip out their throat is just overkill. Or vice versa, the order didn't matter, why keep going after they're already dead?

I grabbed my laptop off the passenger seat to check the national database on the name Charles Brown. I've done this before, many times over the years. It was an exhausting search. But none of the names ever matched. He was a ghost; he didn't exist.

I wish it was as easy as it was in the movies. I'd just go back to a dedicated room in my apartment where I'd have a giant whiteboard with a bunch of names and pictures of murder weapons and crime scene photos taped to it. Everything would be connected by a random colored string, all leading and pointing to a picture of Charlie Brown.

After a few minutes of pacing and mumbling to myself in frustration, I'd tear everything off the board in a rage, crying, as thoughts of the people I've lost flashed through my memory. I'd fall to the floor exhausted, sobbing uncontrollably with my head in my hands. When I finally looked up, I'd notice something I hadn't noticed before. A picture that had accidentally fallen from the board would now reappear, and the lightbulb in my brain would turn on. Slowly, I'd look at that picture, then the picture across the room, and then the picture that miraculously still hung by a tack to the wall. At that point, everything would speed up. Somehow, as if they had a mind of their own, my hands would rearrange all the photos on the board, and I'd stand back and look, finally able to figure it out!

Motivational music would play. The sun would suddenly shine through the curtains, my tears would dry, and I'd have a new lease on life. I'D HAVE A NEW REASON TO LIVE!

But that's just not how things work in real life. In real life, when I opened my laptop, an email popped up from the daughter that I've avoided for the last ten years, wishing me a happy birthday again because she wasn't sure if her texts were going through.

'Hello darkness, my old friend.'

I thought back to the conversation I'd just had with my shrink two hours ago. He seems to think that unresolved issues from my past were finally catching up to me. He thinks that my excessive drinking and isolation all come from the same place. The brain pills I've been taking are just a band-aid over the still-open wounds in my mind.

"Maybe it's time to man up," he said. "Maybe it's time to stop being such a fucking baby."

I admitted that I'd thought about it, calling her and explaining myself. But how? After all this time? I was embarrassed. I am still the lowest form of man. I have absolutely no words to justify putting her through what I put her through. The shame still consumes my entire being.

There are things I'm just not equipped to do.

For instance, I can tell you how it feels to hold a dying man's head in my lap as he takes his last breath, but I can't tell you how to hug your daughter and console her after her first heartbreak.

I can tell you that cutting a man's throat from left to right, as opposed to the other direction will cause a silent scream because of the way air escapes from the windpipe, but I couldn't tell you about the pride a man feels for his child as he lays a valedictorian stole across her neck and shoulders for graduation.

I sat still in the front seat of my vehicle, questioning everything. How do I even start that conversation? What if I reach out and she rejects me? How do I explain that I'm afraid to fail her again?

'Maybe you should stop being such a fucking baby.'

The doc was right, I picked up my phone.

"Hey Karma, it's me, Dad."

Chapter 6: Goddamnit!

"OH MY GOD! HAPPY BIRTHDAY!!" she squealed. "How's it feel to be the big 5-0?"

"Ha ha. I'm not sure yet. It hasn't sunk in," I replied, trying to sound confident while cautiously waiting for the verbal beating I deserved. "My knees hurt. My back aches. I just chased 3 young whippersnappers off my lawn with my cane..."

"Ha ha ha ha! You've always had bad knees. Who are you kidding? You've been old for 20 years! Ha ha ha," she laughed.

It was a beautiful sound. I wondered if I should just come out and say something about the past, or wait and continue our banter. I decided to just go for it.

"Hey, Karma, listen. I…"

She cut me off, "Oh my God! I almost forgot. I made detective!"

"What?!" I tried to match her excitement. "That's incredible! Good job! How do you like it? Who are you working with? Wait, for which department? That's awesome!" I hadn't heard anything about it. It was probably in one of the texts I never read. I'm a terrible person.

I enjoyed listening to her speak. I was grateful that her words were like a run-on sentence as she told me about her life. Fact after fact, rapid fire. I wouldn't have been able to get a word in even if I wanted to.

She had a gigantic personality. There was so much energy coming through the phone that I felt claustrophobic sitting in the front seat. I opened my door and got out.

Still listening, I looked around the parking lot. Aside from a ridiculous looking Cybertruck and police vehicles, there were no other cars. I looked at my watch. 9 am, where were all the workers that should've been here on the job? I noticed that there were no cameras mounted to any of the temporary light poles on site. This was the perfect spot to dump a body.

I covered the mic on my phone and motioned to get a uniformed officer's attention.

Meeting him halfway across the parking lot, I mouthed a question that he couldn't understand.

"Dad? You still there? Did you hear me?" Karma asked.

"Yes," I lied. "Yes, I… " I turned my attention back to the officer. "GODDAMNIT, WHO'S PIECE OF SHIT TRUCK IS THAT?" I blurted out, unnecessarily aggressive. I was frustrated in the moment by doing two things at once, knowing I should've only been paying attention to my daughter.

"I'm sorry, Karma, I'm sorry. These guys… They won't…" I started to explain. I waved the cop over to my car while I spoke to her, "Go ahead, I'm sorry. You were saying?" And she started right back where she left off as I scribbled a note on a receipt.

'Get the 360-degree video from the truck! Asap!' I wrote.

I knew from experience that those vehicles had 24-hour, full car surround cameras and could hold a clue to who dropped off Tyra and her boyfriend in the dumpster.

I remembered a case where a man thought he'd committed the perfect crime.

He'd gotten into a fight with his wife's ex-husband over politics, of all things, and the fact that the ex owned a Tesla and supported the company's owner drove the husband over the edge. They got into a fistfight, and the husband beat the other man to death with his bare hands. Panicked, he dragged the dead man into the garage, cut the body into pieces, wrapped them in plastic, then drove the Tesla around the city, disposing of the body parts in different locations before driving the Tesla over a cliff into the ocean.

Of course, the man's family called, reporting the man missing, and he wasn't hard to find. Not only did the Tesla have GPS to its exact position, it had the recording of the whole fight, murder, and body part disposal sites. They were all perfectly stored in 1080p hi def video, in the cloud.

It was one of the easiest cases I was ever assigned to, and the fact that the husband's hatred of the vehicle was the reason he was caught was just icing on the cake. I remember the judge staring at the defense team with a look of...

"DAD! That's ok, right?" Karma had been speaking the whole time.

"Yes, honey, yes. No problem," I had trailed off in my own thoughts and had no idea what I was agreeing to.

"Ok! I'll send you the address. I'M SO EXCITED! Bye, Dad!" she said.

"Ok, sweet girl, goodbye," I replied. Before I pressed the end call button, I heard my daughter scream "Aaaaaah! Oh my god, oh my god, oh my god!" squeals of joy, as she probably thought she'd hung up already.

I smiled too. I had a long way to go, but I'd taken the first step.

'Dad, my phone's dying! If I don't answer, it's because it's dead and I lost my charger. See you soon!'

I was 4 hours into a 5-hour drive, headed to where Karma lived. We'd planned to meet at IHOP at exactly 8 am.

That's what I had unknowingly agreed to the day before on the phone… to go visit her for a week and have breakfast together every morning.

The ride wasn't bad, even though I hated long road trips. I'd googled things to do on a long drive before I left, and listening to audiobooks was the most recommended suggestion. I picked a story by an author whose name I overheard in the precinct's break room, William something.

I listened to a story called Sins of the Gender about a man who's been continuously let down by the women in his life, which causes a deep distrust and even hatred for them, but he can never just stand by as a female is being threatened or mistreated. Tough guy with a heart of gold.

It was a good story. The author was really clever with how he secretly wrapped a love story inside an action novel.

I was actually in a good mood. There was a nervous excitement running through me. I took a quick glance at the clock. Yep, still had plenty of time.

Chirp! The police scanner I keep in my car alerted me that it had acquired a local signal. I didn't even know what city I was currently in, but I turned up the volume out of boredom. Plus, I was being a little nosy, trying to listen in on the type of stuff the locals had going on.

'Eastbound I-90… Speeds approaching 100mph… slower traffic ahead…'

I saw it as I was hearing it. I was on Route 90 headed in the opposite direction. A helicopter zoomed past overhead. A blue Dodge Charger was being chased by a whole fleet of police cruisers.

A quick search told me the suspect had committed a mass shooting at a school, and there might be children in the car. It started as a domestic dispute. Luckily for me, this wasn't my fight. They were going that way. Until they weren't. I saw them pass on the other side of the road, then as I watched in the rear view mirror, I saw the Dodge get rammed from behind and spun around. Its driver came out of the 180-degree spin, now coming my direction, cutting across the freeway, driving west. The cops tried to follow his path but ended up crashing into each other, leaving a mess of twisted metal just like they always do in the movies. Only the helicopter and a lone cruiser chased him now.

Common sense told me to pull over and let them pass. I was on my way to see my daughter. She was waiting for me. She'd been waiting for 15 years! Just pull to the side, get out of the way, I decided, this wasn't my fight. And that's exactly what I was going to do.

I'd been riding in the left lane, watching as much behind me as ahead, and was just pulling past an 18-wheeler on my right. As the Dodge pulled closer, I put my blinker on and pulled in front of the truck. At the last second, right as the Dodge was ready to pass, I cut back into the left lane. The Dodge hit the brakes and swerved into the median, but quickly regained its composure and tried to pass me again. I stayed with him, forcing him back onto concrete, stuck behind me and the truck. He flashed his lights and honked his horn, swerving back and forth, trying to get around. The helicopter was right above me, though I couldn't see it. The cruiser stayed a safe distance back, but I'm not sure why.

I picked up my police radio and called out as a civilian, saying that I had the guy pinned in, but needed someone to come get him. The woman on the dispatch said there were no more available cars, but that state police are on their way. She told me to stand down and let them deal with it.

POP! POP! POP!

The Dodge had pulled up beside me and was shooting.

Smash! My rear window exploded.

I sped up to get away from him, and as I did, he snuck in between me and the truck and got in the right lane. I cut my wheel hard just as he passed, clipping his driver side rear quarter panel, sending him spinning across both lanes into the grass on my left.

The truck slammed on its brakes and jackknifed, causing it to flip and come apart, dumping its cargo, a farm-load of live chickens, scattered all across the road.

I pulled up close to the Dodge. I had a half-second debate with myself to just continue on down the road; this wasn't my fight, but the thought of potential children in that vehicle overruled all of that.

I glanced at the clock. I still had time. I reached for my Glock…

POP! POP! POP! More shots. The Dodge opened its driver's side door, then closed it and took off.

I stepped on the gas but caught a glimpse of something pink. Two little girls with their little Barbie backpacks stood in the grass where the Dodge had just left, crying. They held hands and looked around, scared. I watched in disbelief as the Dodge sped off, angry that I let him get away, feeling like any more damage done by that asshole would be charged to my failure.

I went to the two crying children and did my best to comfort them as I called dispatch. I looked at my watch. 7:30. Goddamnit! If I left now, I could still make it.

I looked around for the cop who had stayed back. I couldn't see his vehicle past the overturned big rig and the thousands of chickens running around like, well, chickens with their heads cut off. The helicopter left and followed the suspect.

I hurried the girls into my car. I figured I'd just take them to a local police station or the nearest hospital.

"Siri! Navigate to the nearest police station!"

I started the engine and waited for direction. No response. "SIRI GODDAMNIT! NAVIGATE TO THE NEAREST POLICE STATION!" Still nothing. I had no signal. Zero bars. My phone was useless. "FUCKING AT&T!" I grabbed the police radio.

Me: Dispatch! This is Detective Dewayne Lucas. The Dodge got away on Highway 90, westbound. The helicopter is in pursuit.

Dispatch: Yes, we know. Good copy.

Me: Suspect abandoned two schoolchildren. I have them with me. Where are the responding officers?

Dispatch: Who is this?

Me: Detective Dewayne Lucas.

Dispatch: …

Me: Come back, dispatch. Who's coming to get these kids? Or I can bring them to you, either way. Please advise.

Dispatch: Ummm, we don't have a Detective Dewayne Lucas…

Me: (Irritated, I walked away from the car so the kids wouldn't hear me cuss.) GODDAMNIT! I HAVE TWO SCARED LITTLE GIRLS IN THE BACK OF MY FUCKING CAR! I'M NOT FROM HERE, I'M JUST PASSING THROUGH! I'M NOT A BABYSITTER! I HAVE SOMEWHERE TO BE!

Dispatch: We have units on the way. Traffic is blocked in both directions. Stay with the children. Do not leave the crime scene.

Me: No! I'm not staying. I'm leaving. I'll just drop them off.

Dispatch: DO NOT LEAVE THE CRIME SCENE! I REPEAT, DO NOT LEAVE THE CRIME SCENE! YOU WILL BE CHARGED IF YOU TAKE THOSE CHILDREN. ARE WE CLEAR, DETECTIVE?

I got back in my car and looked at the time. 7:49.

"goddamnit…"

Chapter 7: IHOP

Karma was still sitting in a booth at IHOP when I got there at 11:35. I called and texted several times once I finally got signal, letting her know what happened, but I still felt guilty. The truth felt like lies.

She looked like she'd been crying, but put on a brave face as I walked into the restaurant. She stood, ran to me, then jumped into my arms and squeezed me with an urgency that said she was afraid to let go for fear that I might leave again.

"I'm so sorry, baby."

I said it as an apology for today, but meant it as an apology for her entire life. "Come on, let's sit. What's good here?" I asked, as if I didn't already know. I sat opposite where she'd been sitting, but she squeezed into the booth next to me instead, wrapping both of her arms around my one, speaking rapid fire, just like she did on the phone.

Without looking at a menu, I said, "I'm gonna have the French…"

"Toast with extra butter, and hash browns, but not on the same plate!" She finished my sentence for me with a giggle. "I know, I remember. I order the same thing. Every single time!" We shared a laugh, then sat in the moment, allowing it to breathe.

The waitress came with coffee and took our order. I filled our cups, then picked up the sweetener tray and set it on the table in front of us. We spoke at the same time.

"One cream, one pink, one blue! Ha ha ha!" Yes, this is my daughter! We hugged and laughed.

"Wait," I said, as I turned to her and held up both hands. She didn't hesitate. We went through the same elaborate handshake that we made up when she was 10 years old, perfectly, as if we'd been doing it every day for years. Another laugh, and another hug. "Hey. Listen," I said. It was time.

I asked her to get back on the other side of the table so I could look her in the eyes while I spoke. I could feel her reluctance. She didn't want to do this as much as I didn't, but it had to be done. I owed her this. She deserved an explanation. She deserved the opportunity to ask any and every question she wanted to. She deserved to see me uncomfortable, groveling, and embarrassed. She needed to see me be remorseful and vulnerable, honest and apologetic.

So that's what I gave her. I explained what happened at the cliff. I told her how her memory was correct, and I was wrong when I said that she'd misremembered the events of that day. I explained that my distance was out of sheer embarrassment and that my way of coping with that shame was to run away and hide like a coward. I had laid the weight of my failure as a man at the feet of a child, and it wasn't fair. I was and still am disgusted with myself. (I left out the parts about my failed suicide attempts and how I tried to drown myself in copious amounts of alcohol.) I explained how the more time that passed without me fessing up, the more I felt I couldn't come back.

I wanted to shed a tear as proof of my sincerity, but I couldn't let her see me be weak again.

I also explained why I never told the press about Charles and why I took the credit for solving the murders, blaming Jhonny when I knew it wasn't him. I told her that I wanted Charles for myself. I didn't care about the fame or any of the stuff that came with it, I wanted to deal with him for myself.

I held her hand as I spoke. I did my best to answer her unasked questions. I was open to listening to her feelings, ready for her to unload the years of anger and loneliness on me. It was my name tattooed on the scars of her sadness. I'm the bad guy. I made my only child the victim.

I promised to do better. I told her that I couldn't change the past, but I could help sculpt the future if she'd trust me enough to let me try.

She nodded but didn't speak. It looked like she was processing everything in her mind. I spoke softly, "I know we're not gonna fix everything right here and right now. Let me just…"

"How did you and Mom meet?" Karma interrupted me with a question I wasn't ready for. I sat back and smiled at the memory before I began, "Well… It was a clear black night, a clear white moon, ha ha ha…" I said.

I met Keisha while I was still in the academy. I was doing part-time security at a club where her and her friends liked to hang out at. Most people remember her as being mean, but she wasn't, at least not back then. Back then, she was just direct. And like most love stories, she didn't like me too much at first.

She was such a beautiful girl, but she didn't really think that way. She was just so used to having people tell her that she was, it just became an expectation that anytime a man was around, he would be attracted to her.

It was almost like the body dysmorphia that bodybuilders have. You can compliment their biceps all day, but when they look in the mirror, all they see is the skinny nerd they used to be, BUT that doesn't stop them from wearing sleeveless shirts every day.

Anyways, her and her friends would come in, get drunk, and some guy would be too aggressive, so I'd step in and make sure they were safe. Rinse, wash, repeat.

She called me Hero. That was my nickname. "Heeey Hero!" they'd say every time they walked in. I got into a ton of fights because of her. We became friends, but nothing romantic. It wasn't until I had finally become an officer before all that started.

I was a rookie on my first domestic call. Some guy roughed her up, and she was still crying when I got there. The guy was apologetic and admitted that things got out of hand, but swore up and down that he didn't hit her. She called him a liar, and he got up, angry, so I jumped on him and beat him down. Yes, I went too far, it was definitely police brutality, but back then, we didn't get in trouble for stuff like that.

I still remember her voice that day. "Hero? Is that you?" We started dating, got married, and had a beautiful little girl.

"Me!" Karma squealed.

"Yes, you!" I smiled and reached out to squeeze her cheek. "I named you Karma because I felt like you were the reward for all the good I tried to put out into the world. You were the 'thank you' for all the people I've helped. What comes around…

I didn't tell her that Keisha had gone back to drinking and was a terrible version of herself at the time of her murder. I wasn't Hero to her anymore, I was Asshole. Or I was Little pussy man, or Shitbird. She hated me when she passed… I didn't cry at her funeral.

Beep beep beep! A text. Damn phone.

Beep beep beep! A second text. Fuck.

Beep beep beep! A text on Karma's phone, which had been plugged into the outlet, recharging on the table next to us.

Beep beep beep! "JESUS! WHAT? WHAT THE HELL IS SO DAMN IMPORTANT!" I growled, picking up my phone and almost throwing it across the room. Karma smiled a knowing smile and reached to read her own message.

"What the hell?" I said, reading, then re-reading the text. I held up one finger to my daughter, then dialed the call back number.

"What the hell is all this about?" I asked Lieutenant Dan when he answered. "What do you mean, did I kill a suspect? What suspect?" Karma watched as I spoke. "A blue Dodge. Yeah. I slowed the guy down and called it in. No. I stopped to take care of the little girls he'd left on the highway. I called it in on the radio." I was irritated to have to have this conversation.

"He, what? Murdered? NO, I STAYED WITH THE LITTLE GIRLS! THEY TOLD ME TO STAY WITH THE LITTLE GIRLS!"

Apparently, the guy driving the car stopped at a little motel off the freeway to get something from his room, and the cleaning ladies found him lying on his stomach, but face up on the bed. Whoever killed him twisted his head all the way around and stuffed his mouth with soap and toilet paper. He had several different-sized kitchen knives stuck in his back, and a plunger had been shoved violently up his rectum. The guy's underwear was soaked with blood. I was the last person to see him alive, so this police department called the department I'd been consulting with and told them I shouldn't have been working in their district, but still said I should've stopped the guy and brought him in. I was not to follow him and kill him in his motel room.

Lieutenant Dan said he was about a half an hour away and wanted me to meet him at the hotel.

"Wait, do what? For what? Goddammit, Dan, I'm with my daughter. Ok... Ok, fine... Alright." I finished the conversation and tossed my phone down, then looked at Karma, "Lieutenant Dan says hi."

"Lieutenant Dan... Ice cream!" She said with a laugh, then pushed her phone over to me. "Work just texted me too. They want to talk to you about what happened this morning."

Chapter 8: Kitty Kat, don't call me fat

I agreed to follow Karma to the motel, but not before she said, "Dad, there's something I've been wanting to talk to you about, but it can wait till later."

"You sure? Cause we can do it right now. I'm not worried about work, they can kiss my ass," I replied, genuinely concerned with whatever she needed.

"No, it waited this long; a few more hours won't change anything."

Her response stung a little, but she was right.

After an exhausting chase, with me doing my best to keep up with her erratic driving style, we made it to the crime scene on the side of the freeway. She drove the exact same type of F150 that I used to drive when she was young. Same color and everything.

This was her crime scene, and she went to work as soon as we stepped onto the property. I was amazed to see how quickly she went from my daughter to a lead detective, introducing me as Detective Lucas, instead of 'my dad'. Most of the responses were, "I've heard a lot about you," as I shook hands.

There were a few investigators that I'd worked with in the past from different departments on different cases, which wasn't uncommon in this profession. It's always good to have a familiar face to help navigate through the red tape and politics of a specific region.

"Is that my main shit stain, Dewayne?" A female voice called out from behind me.

"And is that, Kitty Kat, don't call me fat, I'm big boned, Thomson!" I called back before turning around. We said the *'I'm big boned'* part in unison.

I was greeted with a hug from one of my oldest friends in the world, Katrina Thomson. She'd always been a very large woman, but where she used to be Lizzo big, she was now more Ashley Graham. I used to date her sister way before any of this police stuff, and we'd been friends ever since, reconnecting randomly throughout the years. I was the best man at her wedding after finding out that she was engaged to my best friend from the police academy, Billy Jo Thompson (Billy Ro). All of it was completely coincidental and a real example of the 'it's a small world' saying.

"Captain? You're Captain Thomson now?" I asked with a smile after she finally let me go.

"You see the hat, right? You see the stripes?" She replied and spun, showing off her uniform sarcastically.

"I do, ha ha, and you look good! You must be on that meth diet. Let me see your teeth!" I laughed.

"Aww, it's so cute that your daughter is taller than you. We should all have someone in the family we look up to. Ha!"

That was our relationship. We teased each other in the most disrespectful ways, but still with so much love and admiration for one another, the same way that siblings do. I was relieved that she was Karma's captain. I hadn't even gotten to the stage where I was worried about her work environment yet.

"How the hell have you…" she started to say before her attention was taken away by a Cybertruck cutting across the parking lot.

"HEY!" she yelled, walking towards it, " GET THAT MOTHERFUCKER BACK BEHIND THAT TAPE!"

Everyone turned to see the commotion. Captain Thomson had a loud, commanding voice; there wasn't a subtle bone in her body. The truck lowered its window just a crack, then reversed and followed the Captain's direction and parked. She walked back, shaking her head, clearly irritated.

"He's here for you," she said, standing next to me.

"Me? What the hell for? I don't…" I watched as Lieutenant Dan got out of the Tesla, check his appearance in the window, then walk towards me wearing his own look of irritation.

We shook hands as I introduced the two of them. Karma walked over, and I introduced her as well. After a quick round of fake pleasantries, we walked into the motel room.

My first instinct was to cover my daughter's eyes and pull her out of the room. The smell of blood and feces made everyone gag. The sight of the man's soiled underwear, plus the plunger pointing straight up towards the ceiling, would've made an inexperienced stomach purge itself right there.

I saw what I needed to see and walked out of the room, then looked around the walkway. I didn't immediately see any cameras, but that didn't mean they weren't there. Karma walked up beside me.

"You ok?" She put her hand on my shoulder, concerned. I appreciated the irony.

"I talked to some of the guys, turns out, he wasn't the shooter," she continued. "The school's video shows the shooter getting into a different vehicle where he was found dead in the front seat. It was parked next to where the blue Dodge was parked. The blue Dodge was just in the wrong place at the wrong time, poor guy was just picking up his daughters. Someone thought he was the killer. They thought they saw something, and you know, people are just… You know, they mean well."

"So, why run then? Why the whole chase?" I wondered aloud, running through the different scenarios in my head.

"Someone else was in the car," Captain Thomson chimed in. She'd walked up behind us. "One of the little girls talked. She said there were people in the car telling her daddy to drive fast."

"Sooo, the little girls just escaped? How's that happen?" Lieutenant Dan joined the conversation.

"No, they were let out," I answered, "I saw the car stop. They were intentionally let out, then the car drove away."

"That's just it," Kat added, "the girl said that the nice lady made the men stop yelling. She made them stop and let 'em out."

We all stood in silence before Karma finally said, "I'm going to check if these security cameras actually work," then walked away. The captain followed.

Lieutenant Dan took a step forward. "Can you imagine? I couldn't... I mean, there's no way I could just leave my daughter's alone like that. No fucking way." He had his head down as he spoke. "They would've had to kill me. As a man, there's absolutely no way I would ever leave my daughters. No way."

Chapter 9: Chopped Champion

We cooked dinner together at Karma's apartment. I did the steaks, she did the potatoes, and we bought a premade bag of Caesar salad. I didn't ask how she wanted her meat cooked, and she didn't ask how I wanted my potato dressed. We didn't need to.

Conversation was light as we spoke casually about everything, work included. I told her some stories about me and Captain Thomson from back in the day. She told me about whatever random thought popped into her head. It didn't get serious until we sat down at the table to eat.

"So…," she started, then stopped. She stared at me, unsure of how to proceed. I tried to soften my features to make her more comfortable. I was ready for it. I deserved what was coming.

"Go ahead," I said, preparing for the emotional explosion.

"I caught him," she said, "I had him." She kept her eyes down, avoiding mine.

"Who?" I was confused.

"Him!" She finally looked up and wiped away tears.

"Charles? What? Where? How? I don't understand," I reached out to grab her hand, which she instinctively pulled away, before allowing it to be held. I was completely lost in the conversation.

"You didn't answer!" Karma burst into tears. I got up, went around to her side, and hugged her. She cried like a child into my chest.

"I'm so sorry," I said, doing my best imitation of what I'd seen other fathers do. I rocked her gently and stroked her head patiently.

When her crying slowed down, she spoke. She told me about meeting her best friend in the entire world, Patricia Brown, at work, and how she and Patricia were bounty hunters. She said that she wanted to be a detective like I was, but could never pass the exam, so the bounty hunter thing was all she could do to bring people to justice, but Patricia was often too rough with the people they would catch.

She paused and sat back to look at me when she said the words, 'too rough', which told me there was more to that statement, but I didn't ask, figuring she'd eventually get to that part.

She told me that there was another girl named Celeste who was part of their gang.

"Wait," I had to stop her there, "You were in a gang?"

She explained that she was in the Avengers, which was their gang name, but they weren't a gang; it was just a joke between them, and she, Karma, was Carol Danvers. She said that even though she and Peppermint Patty were best friends, she didn't know much about the woman's personal life until Celeste was murdered. Come to find out that it was Patricia's husband who did it!

I saw where this was going.

Karma continued in her rapid-fire, run-on sentence way of talking, saying that Patricia's husband's name was Charles. Charles Brown. Charlie Brown and Peppermint Patty. It was like the comics I used to read to her, but she figured it out, and when she called me to ask for advice, I didn't answer!

That's started a whole new round of tears before she started again, saying she'd caught them and was taking him to jail, then Patricia shot that liar, Detective Manny, in the face, then there was a car crash with some milk stealing bitch in an orange car, and the next thing she knew, she woke up in a hospital bed all by herself. Charles and Patricia were gone, but everyone had heard the story, so she finally made detective, and everyone knew who her dad was, but now I was there, and she doesn't want me to leave her again.

My shirt was wet with tears.

As I listened, I saw her mom in her. They sounded so much alike. I'd always had to use my detective skills whenever Keisha was emotional and trying to explain something. It was like her brain would spit out random fragments of thoughts all at the same time, in no particular order, leaving me to have to piece together the full story. I remembered the first time I said, "Keisha, stop! You're giving me a headache!" That was a mistake.

When Karma stopped talking, she looked up at me, waiting for a reaction.

"I fucked up, I'm sorry," I said. It was all I had. Deep down, I wanted her to scream at me. I wanted her to punish me for being the coward I was. I wanted that verbally abusive part of Keisha to come out right then and there, calling me a little pussy boy, and a deadbeat dad who cared more about saving other people than saving his own family. I wanted her to say that I was a piece of shit. An embarrassment. A fucking failure. A scared little man in a boy's body, but she didn't. She didn't need to. We sat in silence as I did it to myself.

"You want a beer?" She broke through the quiet, again proving that she was the more emotionally mature person between the two of us.

Without waiting for an answer, she wiped her eyes, stood, and then grabbed two bottles of Dos Equis out of her fridge. I wiped my own eyes while her back was turned, pretending to be strong.

"2 X's?" I asked with a smile.

"Huh?" She looked at the bottles, but didn't get the joke.

I went into my overnight bag, grabbed a deck of cards, then held them out for her to see. "You remember how to play?"

"Do you?" she replied arrogantly, pulling her hair back, ready for battle.

Her mood changed instantly. She cleared the table, and I turned on the TV to Food Network so we could watch Chopped as background noise.

This is what we used to do. Play Gin Rummy and watch our favorite show. It was like I'd stepped into a time warp. I was lost in the nostalgia of playing games with my little girl, and it felt fantastic! I did my best to keep my normal demeanor on the outside, even though I was ecstatic on the inside. We always played 'the first to five wins is the Chopped Champion,' which was the ultimate championship of all championships, regardless of whatever game we played.

And that was usually me.

We shared information about Charles. I told her that I didn't know about his wife, but it made sense now, considering I'd already thought that at least two people were doing the murders back in my area. I sent a text to Captain Kat, who responded with her approval to me working with Karma on the case.

"I let you win because you're a terrible loser," I said, after she won game 5.

"Chopped Champion! The queen is back!" She bowed her head, and I placed an imaginary crown on it.

"Good job," I said sincerely.

After a gentle back and forth about where I would sleep, I became the chopped champion of sleeping on the couch, then fell asleep happily for the first time in a long time.

Beep Beep Beep! Beep Beep Beep! Beep Beep Beep!

I woke up irritated. I know there's some kind of sleep option on my damn phone… I need to—

"Dad! You see this?" Karma called from the other room. She'd gotten the same texts.

"Yeah!" I yelled back, before mumbling to myself, "I hear these incompetent assholes!"

She'd already had coffee made for us and was sitting at the table, ready to go, by the time I put my shoes on.

"Hold up," I said, as she reached for the door to leave. I ran back to my bag and put on some deodorant.

"Wait, what? What happened to, 'I don't sweat, I'm too cool?'" she mocked with a laugh.

"I got old," I conceded.

"Come on, old man," she said, half hugging me as I walked past.

"You want to drive?" We said it simultaneously. "No! You go ahead, ha ha ha." Again, at the same time.

"What the…?"

She saw it before I did. All four of her tires had been slashed. I looked at mine. All of those had been slashed, too!

A million different thoughts ran through my head. It couldn't be--

Pop! A gunshot.

Pop! Pop! Pop! Pop! Pop!

"GET DOWN!" I jumped to cover my daughter, then scrambled back to the cover under the stairs of her apartment's walkway.

"WHAT THE FUCK? WHAT THE FUCK! WHO'S DOING THAT? WHAT'S GOING ON! FUCK YOU MOTHERFUCKER! FUCK YOU!" Karma yelled as she jumped back into the open, pulled out her service pistol, and let off multiple shots in multiple directions.

"KARMA, GODDAMNIT! STOP!" I yelled, pulling her back to cover. "STOP! You don't even know what you're shooting at! Stop it!"

"No. Dad. I got it. They're trying to kill you. I'll kill them. I'll kill everyone. No. I hate people who kill people. Are you ok? Are you hit? Fuck them. FUCK YOU, MOTHERFUCKERS!" She was acting irrationally.

"KARMA! STOP! LOOK AT ME! HEY, LOOK AT ME!" I grabbed her face. "HEY, calm down, love. Breathe."

"BUT..."

"Karma… Hey. Breathe, take a breath. I need you with me, ok? Alright? Now, did you see where the shots were coming from?" I asked calmly, but urgently. She shook her head no.

"Ok… So, let's figure it out," I said. "How many shots did you count?"

"A hundred," she said, still breathing too fast for my liking.

"No… Think about it. Calm down and think. How many?"

She stopped, closed her eyes, and counted to herself. "6!"

"Ok, good. Me too. Now listen, and look." I pointed at the cars in the parking lot and directed her eyes to the 6 holes in the different vehicles. "So if we can see the bullet holes, where are the shots coming from?" I asked her.

"Above us?" She replied, unsure of her answer.

"Karma. Think. Where did they come from?"

"Above us. We gotta go up from the back and kill those motherfuckers," she growled angrily, jumping up, trying to run that way.

I grabbed her. "Hey! Karma, calm down. Call for backup."

"But "

"GODDAMMIT! STOP QUESTIONING ME! CALL EM!" I demanded, looking back and forth, watching both sides of the walkway. I had my pistol drawn, ready to shoot.

I saw a Cybertruck pull into the parking lot on the opposite side of where we stood, behind us.

Lieutenant Dan.

"Karma, listen, look. There's the lieutenant. Go, get in the truck," I said.

"No, Dad, what about you?" she cried back.

I grabbed her by the arm and dragged her to that side of the building. "Those trucks are bulletproof. I'm right behind you, get in the fucking truck! GO!"

As she contemplated doing what I said, I ran back to where we started. I wanted to lure the gunfire in my direction, so she could get into the electric vehicle safely. "Go!" I yelled, shooting two shots into the air as I saw the Cybertruck's passenger door open. She ran towards it.

POP! POP!

Gunshots ricocheted off the ground next to me. I jumped back into cover.

Then, **POP! POP! POP!** From the Cybertruck.

I watched in horror as Karma got lifted off her feet and blown backwards. She landed flat on the concrete, shot from the front.

"NOOOO!" I squeezed off al 15 shots at the Tesla.
"NOOOO!" I ran to her. It felt like I was moving in slow
motion.

I caught a glimpse of Lieutenant Dan eating an ice cream
cone as he drove away, then dropped to my knees in a pool of
my daughter's blood.

"Dewayne Lucas!"

I turned to look. Charles and his wife stood on the second-
floor staircase, smiling, with their guns aimed at me. I raised
mine to shoot.

CLICK!

They laughed, then ran off the other way. I started after them.

"DAD, WAIT!" Karma called, begging for me to stay with
her while I gave chase. "dad…"

"DAD! HEY, DAD! Don't you hear that?"

"Huh?" I jumped up out of sleep and looked around, unsure of
where I was at first. I heard the text alerts, then I heard the
police sirens.

"You're not gonna believe what happened! Come on, there's
been another murder. I got your coffee on the table!" Karma
said, with way too much energy.

I sat up, grabbed my phone, and asked, "Why are you so wide
awake so early.

"I couldn't sleep. I had the craziest dream," she replied, "then, this happened!"

She ran across her living room and ripped open the blinds in dramatic fashion. When my eyes finally adjusted to the sunlight coming in, I saw a squadron of emergency vehicles and first responders scattered around her parking lot, scurrying around like ants in all different directions. News cameras and Karma's nosy neighbors only added more chaos to an already chaotic scene.

I looked at my phone and saw a text that Captain Thomson sent, asking how long it would take me to get to the address she'd sent.

I responded, 'I'm already here.'

Chapter 10: Endless Knot

I didn't like the feeling I had while climbing the two flights of stairs to the crime scene. I took a left down a long walkway and was hit in the face by the unmistakably heinous stench of death. I covered my nose and mouth with my shirt as I passed the uniformed officers standing near the door. Karma was already inside, talking to her coworkers by the time I'd entered the apartment.

At first glance, nothing jumped out as odd or out of place, and aside from the empty space in the kitchen where a refrigerator would normally be, it looked like any other living space I'd ever seen.

The smell was coming from a different room.

"Detective Lucas."

I ignored Lieutenant Dan's voice as I walked down the short hallway towards the stench.

I passed a regular looking bathroom on my left, and then entered the crime scene on my right.

"FUCK!" I jumped back. It was the first time in a long time that I'd been physically surprised by something. The refrigerator that was supposed to be in the kitchen was here, in the middle of the bedroom. A shirtless man's body hung limp from the upper freezer section. It looked like he'd been looking in the icebox for something to eat when someone came up behind him and slammed the freezer door on his head, then locked it shut.

By the way he hung, I assumed that his neck was broken and the spinal cord had been severed. His body weight was only supported by skin that looked like it'd been stretched to its limit. The man's back had been shaved, and there was a pattern that reminded me of the lattice fence in my grandma's garden, carved crudely into his skin.

He was naked except for boxer shorts and blood-soaked ankle socks, as both his Achilles tendons had been cut.

To the right, against the wall, a dead animal was chained to a bed. It laid rotting in the sunlight that came through the only window in the room.

Poor dog.

That was the stench. The animal had been dead for a long time. It still wore its black collar, with a name tag that read something starting with an S.

As I turned to leave, I saw the same symbol that was cut into the man's body, painted in blood on the wall.

"We're about to pull him down now, detective." Two M.E's from the coroner's office walked in as I walked out.

"I'll be back in a minute," I replied.

"Endless knot," Lieutenant Dan said when I walked into the living room.

"What?" I asked, annoyed.

"The symbol... It means..."

I interrupted him, rudely, by shaking a jar of peanuts that I grabbed off the coffee table.

"Dan. Why are you here? I notice you've been at a lot of these crime scenes lately. Why? Ain't you supposed to be in an office somewhere, telling fish stories, lying about being the hero way back when? Your investigator days have been over for years. What's up, man? What's really going on here?"

He looked hurt.

"I… You know, I just thought…" he started.

This was all too much. This was too close to Karma's home, and mentally, I was at a loss. I felt angry, and I was taking it out on Dan Nash because, well, he was the only one listening. I was upset and lashing out, shooting into a crowd. He just happened to be the one who got hit.

"What's the last case you actually solved, huh? Let's be real, man, why are you here?"

I walked back towards the bedroom, disgusted with myself.

"You remember the Schultz case?" Lieutenant Dan called out behind me.

I did remember.

There was a case years ago where choir boys were being murdered, but there were no suspects and no leads. The press tried to paint it like there was some satanic cult doing it as an offering to the devil, claiming the end of times, and the public ate it up. Religion was at an all-time high. People were looking to be saved. Church was popular again as people went in droves.

We knew better. We had the best and brightest detectives brought in from all over the country, but they yielded no results.

Enter in, Retired special investigator, Monterey 'the Full Monty' Schultz. He was a good guy, known for walking around with his chest out. In today's pronoun world, it'd be called toxic masculinity. Back then, he was Mr. Macho, a man's man. We'd worked together on different cases throughout the years.

By the time of these particular murders, he'd been retired, living his best life, spending most of his time golfing or hanging out with his grandkids, but now, for whatever reason, he was on hand at a lot of these crime scenes. Due to his reputation and the respect that he had within the law enforcement community, he was allowed full access. The man was basically a consultant before consulting was a thing. During one of the briefings, he suggested that a local priest was behind the murders.

Everybody thought he was crazy. The man he accused was a respected guy. He was the people's champ. There was no way that he could do what Schultz accused him of. No way. People took it as blasphemy to even suggest it.

Schultz theorized that the priest was a predator, and knowing that a group of boys were planning to expose him, the priest killed them before they could say anything.

When asked how he figured it out, Schultz, in his moment of clarity and honesty, said that he, too, had been abused as a child. He'd been in a similar situation to the dead choir boys. There were no murders in his case, but there was a plan to expose, and there was pressure to keep quiet. Schultz gave a tearful apology at the press conference for not solving the case sooner.

I assumed Lieutenant Dan was putting himself in the Schultz role.

"What do we got?" I asked, walking into the bedroom, followed by Karma.

The medical examiner team had the man lying on his back, with his head twisted unnaturally to the side. There was a bullet hole between his eyes and more markings across his belly.

The medic closest to me spoke first. "I'd bet money that he was already dead from the broken neck by the time the gun was used on him. The headshot was just overkill."

"And it was done recently," I replied, before adding, "What's that on his stomach?"

"I don't know, but don't it kinda look like the design on Charlie Brown's shirt?" the other medic said.

"Hey! That was my line! He's stealing my words!" Medic 1 said.

"No, you didn't…" They argued like siblings. I turned, looked at my daughter, and walked out.

"Who found him?" I demanded of the officers standing around doing nothing. "Who called this in?" I was met with blank stares.

"Goddamnit, I need some air," I said, then walked outside.

Lieutenant Dan was on my heels, saying something as I closed the door.

"You know what that means, right? That symbol? It's called an endless knot." He spoke to me like I knew what he was talking about. Like he'd shared some great piece of information that was going to fix everything and solve this whole case.

I took a second before I responded. "Look, Dan, I know I went kinda hard on you inside, I'm sorry. My mind is going everywhere right now, but listen, there comes a time in every conversation where you gotta cut the shit and get to the point. Dan, this is that time."

He put his hand on my shoulder and spoke directly. "The endless knot is the Buddhist symbol for Karma."

Chapter 11: Yup

I immediately went and found Captain Thomson and told her to pull my daughter off the case. Karma, of course, angrily objected. It was two against one.

"She's too close," I said, like it was a scripted dialogue. But this wasn't like the movies where something personal happens to a detective and they get sent home because they can't separate the emotional from the mental part of police work. In real life, you do the job you're paid to do.

Frustrated, I walked away, downstairs to Karma's apartment. I needed more coffee.

My angry mind was on Charles. How did he find her? What was his motive? If he wanted to kill her, why didn't he just do it? She would've been an easy, unsuspecting target. Was he there for me? How could he even know I was in town? It'd only been a day and a half.

"I wonder if he saw me on the freeway when he let the little girls go," I said to myself, leaving the apartment and walking out to the parking lot to watch the people out there.

That had to be it, but how much of a coincidence would that be, I thought. I'm just randomly driving down the road, and hear about a kidnapping, and when I try to slow the guy down, that guy just happens to be my eternal nemesis? That's too perfect. It's just too Hollywood.

Well, I continued my thought, coincidences do happen. It's like how Karma just randomly ended up being best friends with her mom's killer's wife, Patricia Brown. I almost didn't believe her when she told me, but there was no reason to lie. She also let me know that her ex, Detective Manny, said that he was only with her because of what I'd done to him years before, when I exposed him as a dirty cop during one of my consulting jobs. She said it was a random event. They'd met when they bumped into each other at a grocery store. He recognized her, saw an opportunity, and ran with it. Coincidences do happen.

I tricked my mind into being satisfied with that explanation. It helped believing in the possibility of chance, because it wasn't like Charles was some criminal mastermind or anything like that. He wasn't a Hannibal Lecter type with this genius IQ, leaving little clues and toying with police. I knew he wasn't out there scheming or planning any of this; he was an opportunist. He acted strictly on emotion. Somebody somewhere pissed him off, or triggered him in some way, and that somebody was murdered because of it. Charles was an impulsive man, and you could tell by the almost careless way in which he left crime scenes. But still, his motives were only known to him.

And that was the exact reason why it's been so difficult to track him down. There was no rhyme or reason that we could figure out for why he did what he did, and who he picked to do it to. It could be man, woman, or child, on any day of any week. It was damn near impossible for us to set up a profile on him because there were no patterns to his crimes. In fact, the only real connection between any of the murders was the sheer brutality of them. The overkillingness of them, if that's even a word.

I walked over to where the news crews were to listen to what was being reported.

One channel said it was a lover's quarrel. A love triangle between this person and the one at the hotel. Another channel said that the landlord killed the man for late rent. A different one said it was a neighbor who killed another neighbor for their barking dog. Luckily, none of them stirred up public fear, saying that there was a serial killer on the loose.

It didn't surprise me, this is how it always was. Even when an official report came out, the media would come up with their own narrative. I walked over to a different reporter who did not have a huge news team behind him. He was doing his interviews on an iPhone, probably some kind of influencer. I eavesdropped on a woman and her husband.

"I seent a man and a lady yelling at each other. Them wasn't no locals either. Ain't never seen 'em round here before. I told Billy, 'looka there, she's hotter than a whore in church', didn't I say that, Billy?"

"Sho did."

"They was just a hootin' and a hollerin', I tell ya what. She was givin him the business cuz he wanted to do somethin and she ain't wanna do it, poor fella. Whatever it was, looked like he was finna cry like lil baby Jesus. I swear I thought I was gone see some big ol crocodile tears. He was poutin like a spoiled child when she screamed bout how she hated him, then she got in their lil buggy and took off! Ain't that right, Billy?"

"Yup."

"The man looked right at me. Looked me straight in my cornea, then went into that building by himself. Looked like the devil, he did, so me and Billy went back to mindin' our own business. We don't like being all in folks business now, do we, Billy?"

"Nope. Sho don't."

I couldn't hear what the reporter asked, but the woman got excited at the next question.

"That's what I said! Ain't it, Billy? I knew it. He looked mad enough to skin a pole cat live! He done killed someone? Is that what this is all about? Fuck around. I thought this was one of those immigrant raids I been hearin about on the boob tube. We thought they was comin to get all them people who drive those electric cars, didn't we? I heard those cars'll give you cancer, and they listen in on everything you say. Ain't nothin private. Them there is spy vehicles, ain't they, Billy?"

"Yup."

"We got a guy who comes around down here all the time. Drives one of those triangle trucks. You ever seen those? Looks like a Star Trek truck. Billy said it looked like a

Battlestar Galactica truck. Ha ha ha. That tickled me silly. Billy ain't never seen no Battlestar Galactica before. I said where the hell did you come up with that from? Fuck around clown. Billy will just say anything sometimes. Ha ha ha, bless his heart."

I interrupted at that point, letting them all know I was the lead detective. "Ma'am, I just have a few questions. Did the woman come back for him? Where did he go? And lastly, would either of you be able to identify the couple if you saw them again?"

They stared back at me like I was speaking a different language.

"Ma'am? Sir?" I pleaded, looking from one to the next.

"We ain't seen nothin, did we, Billy?"

"Nope."

The conversation/argument that started in the car continued in Captain Thomson's office.

"Kat, listen, as a lifelong friend, she needs to be taken off of this case," I begged.

"Captain, no. I'm the only one who knows Patricia. I'm the only one who can stop all of this. I did it before, I can do it again," Karma countered.

"She's too close," I replied, using the same line again. I looked from one to the other. "She needs to be put on paid leave. You need to go on vacation, away from danger. I'll figure this out, and you can come back. Just go somewhere. Stay with friends. Go anywhere else."

"I don't have anywhere else to go," she said, sadly.

The look on her face tore a hole in my soul. The other night, she told me that her grandmother had passed a few years earlier. Keisha's mom was a good woman who raised my daughter in my absence. She was never my biggest fan and made sure to let me know every time we had to communicate.

"Fine," I relented, "but she needs 24-hour protection. You need to have a 24-hour security team with her. Put a uniform with her."

"We can't just take people off the street, Dewayne, you know this."

"I don't need security. I'll be fine. I'm a big girl now, I can handle myself," Karma said defiantly.

"NO!" I raised my voice in frustration, "I want someone with her, full time!"

"Hmm, let me see," Captain Thomson scratched her chin like she was thinking. "If only she had someone who loved her to stay by her side and devote all their time and energy to keep her safe. Someone brave and strong. Someone with experience who's battle-tested and knowledgeable. Dang it, Karma. Didn't we just fire a guy like that? Maybe I could call him and see if he'll come back. Whatcha think? Maybe if we beg…"

"Ha. Ok," I said, feeling foolish, "I just meant… Ha ha, ok, you're right." I shook my head. That was embarrassing. My daughter must think I'm a complete asshole. I changed the subject.

"So, let's go over the facts and just say them out loud so everyone's on the same page. We agree that this is all Charles and his wife, right? We're not thinking of any plot twists or copycats or anything like that, correct?"

They both nodded and said yes. I wrote Charles and Patricia at the top of a piece of paper.

"And even though we don't know if the hillbilly's were telling the full truth, it stands to reason that they were together and probably arguing, if we go by what Karma remembers about their relationship. Right?"

"Right."

"And Karma, you said Patricia was violent, but she was only aggressive towards bad people. People who were proven to have done bad things, other than Charles, of course. But in normal life, she was a good person." I paused to take a breath, and Karma jumped right in.

"Right, which is why I know for a fact that she would never hurt me. She had a chance on that last night we were together. She had a gun! She could've killed me right then and set her husband free, but she didn't. And you heard what they said about letting those little girls out of the car... She's a good person. You guys, trust me on this."

"Unfortunately, we can't trust anyone at this stage." Lieutenant Dan walked into the room after an unanswered knock.

Karma continued, ignoring the older man's words, "And the more I think about it, I don't think she's helping him. They're married, yes, but during my time knowing her, they led two separate lives."

"Times change. People change. It is what it is. We can only go by the facts that we have in front of us," the lieutenant said, determined to have his moment.

I didn't say it out loud, but I had to agree with him. Still, in my own admitted pettiness, I asked, "Hey, there's something else the woman said. She said there was an electric triangle truck that's been riding through their neighborhood lately. Dan, that wasn't you, was it? You drive an electric triangle truck."

The lieutenant looked shocked by my question. He shifted his weight and looked at everyone in the room before answering, "I, um, no. What? I live over 4, um, 5 hours away. How does that..."

"I think that they were arguing about what to do with Karma, and our victim was just in the wrong place at the wrong time," I interrupted, letting the suddenly nervous man off the hook.

My comment made sense to the group as I could see that seedling of thought growing roots inside everyone's head.

"But why? After all this time, why come after her now?" Captain Thomson asked.

"Opportunity. Think about it. If he saw me during the chase. He knew I was in the area. Then, if they were watching at the hotel, she saw Karma. Maybe the wife made a big deal out of her old friend."

"Yeah, maybe she wanted to talk to me," Karma got excited and went into rapid fire mode, "Or said that she missed me. Oh! Maybe she was so proud of me for making detective! She knew how bad I wanted it. She probably made some joke to him about the Avengers and said we should've took him down. Ha ha. She was always such a smart ass. She didn't care what anybody said about anything, she'd always have some wise ass remark waiting. Maybe he got mad at her cuz she likes me better, and he was jealous. She always said that she hated moving so much; she probably wanted to stay and be friends with me again. I remember this one time, she got so mad when I asked if she knew the home improvement lady since they both have the same name, and then the other time when me, her, and Celeste went to Chili's and she was having so much fun with us cuz we were a…"

"Karma, please… Fuck!" Lieutenant Dan put his fingers in his ears and shook his head.

I shot him a death stare. I decided that I was going to kick his ass when all of this was over.

"So what are they driving?" I said, to shift the attention back, "I'm sure they drove stolen vehicles to wherever the crime scenes were, but they can't just be traveling around in stolen vehicles. Do we have any information on that?"

Kat Thomson shook her head, "We got guys checking all the rental companies now."

"That's a waste of time. Come on, everyone, use your brains! What makes you guys think they have to rent? I'm sure they have their own vehicles, and those vehicles are probably not registered to Charles and Patricia Brown," Lieutenant Dan said.

"HEY! ENOUGH!" I yelled. "You're bringing a lot of negativity to this conversation without any answers. Do you have something to contribute, or would you rather complain from outside?" I stood, ready to fight.

"Well, it just seems obvious to me. You know what they look like, do a sketch, pull up some old photos. I know you guys have heard of facial rec. Hell, me and you just used it last month on the Gaines case, Dewayne. If that doesn't work, we go to the press."

Maybe it was all the emotion of the situation. Maybe it was the re-familiarity of being a protective father again. I don't know why I felt the way I did, but the arrogance in Lieutenant Dan's tone during his little soapbox speech was like nails on a chalkboard to me. Then there was something in the way he just walked away, like it was his mic drop moment, that made me want to run after him and punch him right in his stupid looking face.

But I didn't... I couldn't. He was right.

Chapter 12: I can't live

I did my best to keep my emotions in check about the disrespect I felt Lieutenant Dan showed my daughter, but after an hour of biting my tongue, the taste of blood was making me sick. I cornered him in an office, then shut the door and was 10 minutes into a cuss word filled lesson, detailing the dos and don'ts about addressing my daughter, when Karma burst into the room out of breath, saying, "We got 'em!"

I ran to catch up and was followed closely by Daniel Nash. We all jumped into Karma's truck, headed to where the Browns had been spotted. She told us that the facial recognition hit almost immediately, and video from a motel down the road from her apartment showed the couple going into their room.

Every branch of law enforcement was already on scene by the time we pulled up. Captain Thomson had the megaphone, but I convinced her to let me talk. We had everyone strategically in place, armed to the teeth, expecting a gunfight. Charles was not going to go down easily, so a decision had been made to quietly evacuate every room except theirs. The guests would then be gathered and questioned off-site.

At the Captain's signal, a SWAT officer banged on the door. I stood just behind him.

"CHARLES! CHARLES BROWN, COME OUT WITH YOUR HANDS UP!"

Everyone waited with bated breath. No answer, I called out again, "CHARLES AND PATRICIA BROWN! THE BUILDING IS SURROUNDED! COME OUT OR WE'RE COMING IN!" Again, no answer.

With a nod to the SWAT commander, they used a battering ram to smash the door in, then ran inside, guns drawn, screaming instructions.

I followed, my own gun drawn, ready to finally put this chapter of my life behind me. I felt the most satisfying sense of justice as I saw my brother T-Bone, and I saw Keisha, and I saw the hurt of all the families affected. I imagined that this is what people meant when they said they saw their lives flash before their eyes. I saw the end to all of the bullshit Charles had put me through. In those few seconds from the door to the front room, I felt the strangest moment of relief. I actually smiled and was ready to accept peace.

"CLEAR! CLEAR! ALL CLEAR!" Shouts from the SWAT team.

"Wait, what?" I asked, confused as to why the room was empty.

"WHERE THE FUCK ARE THEY?!" I yelled. "WHERE THE F..."

"DAD!"

I looked over at Karma, who was pointing to a door that connected the two rooms. I yanked it open and kicked in the door that was right behind it, as that second room's door had been locked from the other side. That room was empty as well.

I ran out the front yelling at everyone outside, screaming into the megaphone, "WHERE ARE THEY? WHERE THE FUCK DID THEY GO?! WHERE ARE THE PEOPLE WHO CAME OUT OF THIS ROOM? WHERE THE FUCK ARE THEY?! FIND 'EM! NOW!" I saw red. None of it made any sense. I didn't even realize that I still had my pistol out and was waving it around until Lieutenant Dan walked up to me with his hands up.

"Dewayne... Hey, Detective, the gun."

I looked down, holstered it, then continued my rant.

"DETECTIVE LUCAS! ENOUGH! THEY GOT AWAY, SHUT THE FUCK UP!" Captain Kat yelled at me from across the walkway. "Either help us figure it out or bring that nonsense somewhere else!"

I stared anger at her, then walked away and sat on the tailgate of Karma's truck. I watched all of the different agencies gather up their teams, then start the process of packing up and going back to wherever they came from. I just sat there, stewing in my failure. I couldn't help but laugh at myself for getting so emotional about it, I should've been used to it by now. Here I was yelling at people, pissed off at them, when the truth was, it's been me the whole time. I just wasn't very good at my job. Ironically, it reminded me of Charlie Brown trying to kick the football. He tried and tried, but that little bitch Lucy kept pulling it away from him at the last second. Every time you see him lining it up, you're like, "No, Chuck, don't do it! It's a trick! She's just going to get your hopes up, then let you down. Stop, Charlie Brown, just fucking stop!" But what does he do? He foolishly convinces himself that this time will be different. "What a fucking loser," I said to myself.

Done with my pity party, I decided to walk back to Karma's apartment. I needed to pack up all of my stuff. I'd told her that

I'd agree to stop trying to get her taken off the case if she'd agree that we stay anywhere besides her apartment.

"Detective Lucas."

I stopped at the sound of my daughter's voice and saw her walking towards me with a laughing Captain Thomson and Lieutenant Dan. He had his arm around her shoulder, which hopefully meant that he'd apologized to her as I strongly suggested earlier.

I sat back down and waited. My irritation grew at their giddiness in light of this epic failure.

"What the hell is so funny?" I asked.

"Cap was telling us about the way you used to pout when you didn't get your way back in the day," Karma joked, "she said you used to make the exact same face you're making right now. Ha ha ha."

"That's a lie," I replied dismissively.

"Is it?" Kat Thomson laughed. "You don't remember that time we played spin the bottle, and none of the girls would kiss you, so you threw your little temper tantrum, then went and sat in the kitchen? You sat there looking like you were gonna cry... Had your little legs swinging because they couldn't reach the floor. That didn't happen? Ha ha ha."

"Kinda like right now, look at you," Lieutenant Dan added.

I looked down and sure enough...

"Ok, ok. Ha. Ha. Very funny," I said, not finding it amusing at all. "What the hell happened here?"

"Poor police work," Kat said. "Charles and his wife were here, but nobody checked on the room layouts. We didn't know there were connecting rooms. When we did the evacuations, they must've escaped out that next door, and just mixed in with the other guests. Probably wearing disguises. We let them slip through our fingers, and I'd bet everything in your pockets that they're long gone by now. Hell, I would be."

I shook my head in disbelief, wondering how I could be so dumb.

Dan thought the opposite about Charles. He thought they'd stay in the area. He seemed to think that Charles had something up his sleeve. He reasoned that whatever hate he had for me and Karma had not been realized yet. That fire had not been extinguished inside his brain. He likened it to an addict who couldn't rest until that dopamine rush was satisfied.

His theory made sense, and if I'm being honest, I wasn't afraid for me or Karma. I was afraid for everybody else in the world who would ultimately pay for the sins of someone they didn't know. All on the whim of a madman's urges.

The four of us stood around and tossed ideas at each other, brainstorming different strategies and lightly debating what the best moves would be going forward. We watched as the few remaining officers finished up and left at the same time that the residents were finally allowed to return to their rooms.

I decided to call it a night. I physically felt the mental exhaustion as I opened the passenger side door on Karma's truck.

POP! POP! Gunshots.

We all ducked and drew our weapons instinctively, even though the sound came from down the street. Karma drove us all in that direction, towards her apartment.

We listened with trained ears, driving slowly, hoping for something obvious to jump out and lead us to any sort of resolution. We circled the block cautiously until we came back around to where we thought the shots came from.

"HEEELP! SOMEBODY HELP ME! CALL THE 9-1-1. PLEASE CALL THE 9-1-1! IT'S MILLIE!" A hysterical man ran into the road, yelling, banging on the hood of the truck, begging us to stop. He couldn't have known we were cops.

The four of us jumped out and followed him to a patch of grass where a woman's body lay dead, shot twice, once in the head, once through the heart.

"Ow my Gawd! Ow my Gawd! They kilt Millie. They kilt my Millie. I can't... I don't know what to do... I told her don't do the interview today, I told her. But she did it anyways. She did the interview, and the gubberment saw it, and they killed her.

Ow my gawd! What do I do? I can't live. How am I supposed to live? I need to sit down!"

Billy, the husband I had questioned earlier, hurried back into his apartment as Karma, Lieutenant Dan, and Captain Thomson started making calls and securing the scene.

I followed the man to his front door.

POP!

I walked in and saw Billy dead on the couch, with a framed picture of his beloved wife in one hand, and a .45 caliber pistol in the other.

Chapter 13: Relearn how to smile

Nothing happened in the two weeks since the Blunder at the Budget Suites, so after I helped Karma move into a new apartment in a different part of the city, I went back home. In the first couple of months after that, my daughter and I visited each other every weekend, alternating locations, and spoke on the phone at least once a day, every day. The visits eventually turned into plans to meet, and the daily calls turned into texts every now and then. There wasn't any particular reason, or any love lost, it was just how time worked. On a much smaller scale, it's like the saying when someone passes, 'the pain of loss never goes away. It still hurts just as much, but with time, you don't think about it as often.' Eventually, you relearn how to smile.

Plus, her workload had increased. Her department took the Charles Brown stuff to the public. They had his wanted picture on TV, and on billboards, and all over the internet... It was everywhere. They even offered a reward. And Karma was the face of it all. She was the one doing the press conferences. She was the face on TV, the voice on radio, the special guest on all those weird unsolved mystery crime podcasts. (Which I hated by the way. Death and murder are not entertainment. Real crime should not be a best-selling category, and serial killers shouldn't be famous.)

But I digress.

Karma was popular now, and the truth was, she just didn't have time for me. It was exactly what Harry Chapin sang about in that Cats in the Cradle song, back in the 70's.

Charles and Patricia were gone, and while there were still murders every day, it wasn't them.

I'd gone back to drinking by the lake most days and seeing my doctor once a week. He claims to see a difference in me. He'd cut my Zoloft prescription in half, claiming that now, since I've reunited with Karma and let go of some of the guilt I carried around, most of the things I'd complained about were just signs of getting older. "You're at that age, Dewayne, shit happens, quit being a bitch about it. Consider it an honor.

A lot of dead people would kill to have lived as long as you."
It was an odd thing to say, but I get what he meant.

I had just taken a long drink of Dos Equis when I felt something heavy tug on my fishing line, knocking the bottle out of my hand.

"Fuck!"

Beep Beep Beep!

"Really?" I said to myself. I'd forgotten to shut off the ringer. It was Karma. I answered as I tried to reel in Moby Dick.

"Hey, babe!" I said, happily. It'd been a few months since we talk-talked.

"Hey, Daddy! Guess what?" As usual, she didn't give me a chance to answer. "They selected me to be on the show! The same show you were on! 48 Hours! Ain't that crazy? They called to ask me if I wanted to do it, and I was like, 'Who is this?' I thought it was a joke. They're gonna pay me and I'm guaranteed at least 10 minutes of screen time every episode, and I hung up at first cuz I thought it was Captain Thomson playing a trick on me. I met her husband by the way, did he call you? I gave him your number. Nice guy. He told me some funny stories about you guys from the academy. Anyways, the people from the show called back and said they were going to email me some details, which they did, and then they sent a lady named Marcy to come talk to me and showed me everything. Dad? You still there?"

"Yes, love. That's.."

"And then Marcy took me out to lunch at guess where? IHOP! Ain't that funny? Like, who goes to lunch at IHOP? It's a breakfast..."

"KARMA! SLOW DOWN!" I said, smiling to myself. I didn't want to kill her enthusiasm, but there's no telling how long she was going to go on for. "Can we meet? I just want to share some of my experiences I had while doing the show before you commit fully."

"Dad, no. I'm already on it. The first episode airs tonight at 8! I wanted to surprise you. Surprise!"

"Wait, really? What time? 8?" I looked at my phone, 7:15. Ok. I gotta get home. Congrats, I'll call you after."

I cut my fishing line and let the killer whale I had on the hook go, then hurried home.

I called her after the show and congratulated her, calling her a natural and telling her how proud I was of her. She tried to deflect, modestly, saying how she should've said this or that, and she should've had her hair different, and how she wished her mom could've seen it.

"Oh, did you notice I was wearing the infinity pin?" she asked.

I did. It was the hairpin that looked like a sideways 8, which Keisha wore every single day as her way of having Karma close to her. She called it a 'what goes around, comes around' pin. We bought it for Mother's Day.

I went against my instinct, which wanted me to constructively dissect every detail of her police work, from how she addressed suspects to what her body language was saying about her confidence. But this was her moment to shine, she didn't need a life lesson right then.

We spoke. Well, she spoke for hours, and I hung up happy, proud of my little girl.

For reasons I still don't understand, I went to the show's fan page to see how she'd been received as the new cast member.

Bad mistake. The vile shit that was being said about my little girl by these internet trolls was disgusting. The level of disrespect from these people hiding behind their computer screens was incredible. I wanted to respond to every single one of them, promising to do them physical harm for what they'd posted. I wanted to smash their faces with whatever device they used to comment and make them literally eat their words. It reminded me of a quote I'd heard, 'I am all for everyone having a voice, I just don't think everyone has earned the microphone, and that's what the internet's done.'

It's been proven time and time again, the people talking the most noise are the same people who cry the loudest when they need help. There's nothing like hearing tough guys cry.

Frustrated, I threw my phone across the room, got out of bed, and angrily opened a bottle of Tito's vodka. I needed something to take the edge off.

I woke up sitting at the kitchen table wearing a stocking cap, boxer shorts, and one sock with a hole in the toe. My throat felt like I'd been eating sandpaper all night. My head pounded to a beat only I could hear, as the drum major led his line through the halftime show in my skull.

I looked at the clock on the stove through crusted eyes. I was late. I cursed myself for letting somebody's family down in their time of need. I couldn't remember exactly where I was supposed to be that morning, but I wasn't there, and I failed in my commitment to that task.

45 minutes later, after clumsily getting myself ready for the day, I sat in the front seat of my truck, irritated that I had to go back inside after forgetting my phone in my apartment.

"Hey Siri! Where are you?" I yelled, looking around my living room. It wasn't in its usual place on the nightstand. I tried to do a quick playback of the last time I'd had it, and vaguely remembered throwing it somewhere last night.

I found it in a pile of dirty clothes with the ringer off.

I didn't bother looking at the messages as it buzzed with the intensity of a personal pocket massager, waiting until I got back in my truck to check who'd been trying to get a hold of me.

"OH SHIT!"

Every message was some form of, 'Karma's been hurt. Karma's in the hospital. Daddy, where are you? Dewayne, answer your fucking phone, something happened to your daughter!'

I took off like a bat out of hell, driving towards her city. I called Karma's number, but it kept going to voicemail. Then I called the hospital, which put me on hold, so I called Captain Thomson, who answered on the first ring. "Where the fuck have you been, asshole? We've been trying to call you all morning! Who's the lucky guy keeping you up all night?"

"Kat! What happened? Where's Karma?" I wasn't in the mood for banter. "My phone..."

"She's with the doctor now. She was shot, but she had her vest on... Broke a few ribs, I think. They're still doing tests."

"Shot?" My anger went from 0 to 1000. I was ready for war.

"Yeah, she was trying to stop a robbery at a gas station on her way home from work. Some guy tried to carjack the governor's wife. Your daughter caught the guy, but she got hit doing it. They're calling her a hero. The press is here... everybody's here. They're treating her like the Virgin Mary right now, it's crazy. Don't you watch the news? It's been all over TV. It's getting national coverage. Wait. What the hell? OH SHIT! SOMETHINGS HAPPENING! I'LL CALL YOU BACK!"

"NO! WAIT! WHAT'S HAPPENING? KAT! FUCK, KAT!" The line went dead. "SIRI, CALL KAT. NOW!"

"There is no Kat Now in your contacts."

"NO, I'M SAYING KAT THOMSON!" I yelled.

"Now playing Jack Johnson on Apple Music."

"AAAAHHHH! NO. YOU FUCK..." I dialed the number myself, making mistakes as I did, since my fingers decided they didn't want to work right then.

She called me back and apologized for hanging up. "Someone broke through police lines, and everyone panicked. Karma's got armed security now. Ha ha ha. They treating her like Mother Teresa. Hurry up, slowpoke. You need help? I bet they'll give you a police escort." She added that people had been coming to the hospital with flowers and gifts.

"I'm on my way. Hey, have her call me as soon as she can, ok? And keep your phone with you! Put my contact name as Free Food or Pizza Hut Buffet so I know you'll answer," I half joked as my nerves had finally begun to settle.

"Aye aye, Arnold Short-zenneger," she replied without missing a beat.

Chapter 14: Pump the gas

Ding!

"No, we're so close. Just gimme a little more," I said to my truck's gas tank.

The gauge said I had 15 miles of fuel left. Google Maps said I was still 20 miles away with traffic ahead. I saw a Chevron sign and got off on the next exit.

I pulled into the parking lot of what had to be the busiest gas station I'd ever been to. It reminded me of those pictures I saw of the gas shortage back in the 70's. Every pump had at least a 5-car line waiting. I debated parking and going in, but figured the lines inside would be just as long.

I called Kat for an update, and she told me that Karma'd been in and out of sleep. Her breathing had the doctors on edge. She was ok, but they were keeping a very close eye on her oxygen. The governor had been there, and the governor's wife made a statement that as long as Karma was in the hospital, she would be too. I told my friend I was close and thanked her for staying by my daughter's side, knowing that crimes were still happening all over the city. "I mean, someone, somewhere has made too many donuts," I said, "and if you're not there to help, they're going to be thrown away."

"Hey Dewayne, can you do me a small favor when you get here? I need you to bring a step stool so you can climb up and kiss my ass."

"Ha."

As I crept slowly towards my turn at the pump, I remembered the time when me and her...

HOOONK!

"NO! I SAID BUDWEISER, CHELSEA! JESUS CHRIST!" A man yelled to a woman from his car.

"FUCK YOU! I'M PAYING, I'LL GET WHAT I WANT!" she yelled back.

I laughed; she had a point. It's funny how money can change the dynamics in a relationship, depending on the status of said relationship. For instance, if a...

"FUCK YOU, PUMP THE GAS, ERICK! MAYBE IF YOU HAD A FUCKING JOB AND WEREN'T SUCH A WORTHLESS PIECE OF SHIT, YOU COULD BUY YOUR OWN BEER! I'M NOT PAYING AND PUMPING! PUMP THE GAS, ERICK!"

People waiting in their cars started honking their horns impatiently, wanting the couple to either fuel up or get out of the way. I was in a different line, it didn't matter to me. I honked too.

The man jumped out of the passenger side of their Ford Ranger with his middle fingers up to everyone honking, which only made us honk more.

He went around to the driver's side and tried to open the door. The woman had rolled the windows up and locked him out.

"CHELSEA, OPEN THE DOOR!" He yelled, running back to the other side and trying that one. "UNLOCK THE FUCKING DOORS, CHELSEA. NOW!"

I saw people with their phones out, filming the whole scene. The crowd was laughing and pointing, which made the guy even angrier. Someone started a chant.

"PUMP THE GAS, ERICK! PUMP THE GAS, ERICK!"

My line was moving fine, I was one car away.

I watched as Erick ran back and forth, jumping in and out of the bed of the truck, slamming his hands on the hood, all while trying to hold his oversized shorts up, and still giving the crowd the finger. 'Just pump the gas, dummy,' I thought. It was actually pretty funny.

Until it wasn't.

Just as I pulled up to my pump, he grabbed a tire jack, smashed her window, and grabbed her by the hair, trying to pull her from the truck.

I didn't hesitate. I heard sirens as someone must've called the cops already, but this couldn't wait. I was on him in an instant.

A punch to the kidney made him let go of Chelsea's hair. I spun him around and hit him with two quick punches to the face, breaking his nose and jaw easily.

The bigger man jumped at me and was able to get me down, but only because I slipped on the broken glass. We grappled on the ground. Chelsea got out of the truck, yelling every bad thought she'd ever had about him. She grabbed the tire jack and hit him repeatedly. I heard ribs crack, but he kept fighting. I figured he was on drugs. Those guys don't feel pain when they're high; you have to beat them all the way down and restrain them, so that's what I did.

I had him in a rear-naked chokehold, MMA style, when the cops pulled up, ordering me to let him go. I'd already won, but still gave a final squeeze which popped the shoulder out of its socket and snapped his arm in two before I released him. I admit, it was unnecessary. Old habits die hard.

"Thank you, officer. I'm Detective Dewayne Lucas," I said, standing and brushing myself off, reporting what had happened.

In an unexpected turn of events, the officer grabbed me and put me in cuffs. I was being arrested! I couldn't believe what was happening, and despite Chelsea telling them they had the wrong guy, plus the objections from a whole crowd of witnesses, they put me in the backseat of their car and drove away, taking me to jail.

I emphatically pleaded my innocence, trying to explain who I was, where I was going, and what had just happened.

"Call your Captain, call the governor's office," I said to deaf ears. I gave up and sat back, figuring I'd just have to explain at the station.

Sitting at a stoplight, I looked over and saw a Cybertruck pull up next to us.

"Lieutenant Dan!" I yelled. "Hey, that's my lieutenant! Ask him. Ask him who I am. He'll tell you. He's probably going to the hospital right now, just ask him!"

I saw Dan look over at the officer and nod a greeting, but he never looked at the backseat. I wouldn't have either.

I went absolutely bananas at that point. Yelling, kicking, and cussing, trying to get the Lieutenant's attention. He pulled off without another glance.

"Sir, we've asked you nicely, and since you don't want to cooperate, you leave us no choice," the officer in the passenger seat said. The driver put the car in park and they got out right there in the middle of the street, opened my door, hog tied me, and put a gag over my mouth. I didn't fight, I knew that the more I struggled, the tighter the restraints would be.

We pulled off with me thinking about Karma, feeling like a failure once again. We stopped at another stoplight, and I looked over at a sign that said hospital with an arrow pointing to the right. All I could do was hang my head.

Honk! "Let's go, buddy," the officer in my car said to the slow moving traffic ahead of us.

Another Cybertruck pulled up next to us. 'What's with all these...' I started, before I stopped mid-thought, shocked at a sight that took my breath away.

The man in that vehicle was the man I'd been hunting for the last 15 years! He looked right at me just before he turned in the direction of the hospital, and for a split second, we locked eyes. He wore a disguise, yes, but I know who it was, I know what I saw. I saw evil. I saw the devil himself driving with my daughter's 'best friend in the entire world', riding shotgun. As the squad car I was in pulled off towards the police station, I watched helplessly as Charles Brown headed down the road, towards the ER where Karma was.

Chapter 14: Let it go

I was brought back to my car 2 hours later, after Deputy Dickface and Officer Shitbird finally decided to do their jobs and make the necessary calls, proving who I was. When all of this was over, I would be filing a formal complaint to Captain Thomson about the Mayberry style police department she ran, but for now, I kept my mouth shut. I had bigger issues to deal with.

For the sake of being dramatic, of course, my phone's battery was dead when I got in my car. And of course, I didn't have a charger because I'd accidentally left it in Karma's truck and never replaced it. I ran inside the gas station to buy a new one, but of course, they were sold out of the lightning cables that older model iPhones were known for.

It didn't matter, I needed to get to the hospital and talk to Captain Thomson. I jumped in my car and peeled off. I called her on the walkie-talkie and told her to meet me in the lobby. I didn't say why, because I didn't want to put vital info on the air. I couldn't know who was listening.

Ding!

Damnit, in my haste, I forgot to get gas. My car was still on E, but by the grace of whoever you pray to, I still made it.

Kat was waiting where I asked her to when I got there. I pulled her to the side where no one could see us.

"Turn your radio off," I whispered.

She did. I took another look around to make sure we were out of sight before I spoke. "I saw him! He's here!"

"Who's here? And why are we whispering?" she mocked.

I cleared my throat and continued in a louder whisper, "Charles. They were here. I saw them. They didn't go inside? Did you see his wife?"

"No, but I was on the other side of the security area," she replied. "They're still not letting anyone in without credentials, and there's a whole separate area for guests with gifts."

"I saw them in a Cybertruck headed this way when I was on my way to your little podunk jail. I looked right at him. I don't think he noticed me in the back of a police car, though. We need to check all the security cameras, inside and out. Use the facial recognition software. They were wearing disguises, but it was them, trust me. We need to do this now, but quietly, ok? Don't raise any alarms."

"Dewayne, I know how this works," she said.

"My bad, I know you do. I apologize, but this is our chance. They'll never see it coming," I said, ending our secret meeting, then walking back towards my car.

I was excited. I had an anxious energy running through me. All we had to do was find the plates to their vehicle, and Tesla would give us the coordinates to their location. I felt good about it. I was feeling like this time would be different, Lucy be damned. I was finally going to kick the football, and if she tried to move it this time, I'd kick her too.

"Hey. Is there a gas station close by? And do you have a charger?" I kept talking as she followed me outside. "Oh, you still use a Flintstones Android, huh? No problem, I'll just pick one up. One more thing, I'll need another gun. You got something small for my ankle?" I asked, climbing into my front seat.

Captain Thomson didn't answer, she just stared at me in disbelief. She was in shock. I figured she wasn't used to the type of action I'd just thrown at her. I got out, walked over to her, and reached to give her a hug. "Hey, listen. It's sweet that you're worried about me, but I'll be ok."

Oof!

She punched me in the gut unexpectedly and pushed me away.

"Get off me! What the hell is wrong with you?"

"What?" I asked, confused. "Why-"

"Ain't you forgetting something?"

I shook my head, no, not that I could think of.

"Your daughter... Remember her?"

Shit!

I ran back into the hospital, then immediately ran back outside to ask where I was supposed to go. I was a complete mess.

Kat walked up to me and returned the hug. "Hey, friend. Take a breath."

I tried to pull away from her abnormally powerful grip at first, but eventually accepted and appreciated the pause. (Plus, she was a lot stronger than me, I couldn't have gotten away even if I'd wanted to.)

Karma was asleep when I walked in, and the sight of her lying there connected to machines humbled my entire being. Tears flowed freely as every emotion hit me all at once, each one of them fighting for my attention. Helplessness and anger led the pack, with sorrow and regret a close second. I looked around the room at all the flowers and gifts, then searched for doctors or nurses, wondering why there wasn't anyone fixing her right now, wanting to lash out at everyone within earshot, but only seeing Captain Thomson standing in the doorway, watching me, with tears of her own dripping down her face.

"She's alright, she's just resting. Breathe, Dewayne. She's ok."

That's what I needed to hear. I looked back at Karma, who was only connected to an IV machine. That was a good sign, I relaxed a little bit. Well, I relaxed enough to recognize that I was wrong in my earlier thought about loss. Time would not heal anything if something worse than this were to happen and I were to lose her. I would never recover from that. Never. I thought about all the time I wasted, as regret took a commanding lead in the emotion race inside of me.

Anger turned to rage. Rage wanted violence. I wanted the guy who did it.

"NO!" Captain Thomson said it before I even turned around. "I see it all in your posture. Let all of that air out of your skinny little pigeon chest. You are not doing anything to that man. You can't get to him anyway. It's being taken care of, let it go."

"Kat!"

"Dewayne... Let it go."

We stood there staring at each other, when a nurse with good hair appeared and asked us politely to, 'shut the fuck up, and let her patient rest.'

"Y'all take that noise down the hall," she demanded.

I liked her instantly, and was glad she was the one taking care of my daughter. Her name tag read Becky.

Another woman approached, looking at me suspiciously, with an irritated, almost arrogant look about her.

"Miss Garrett, this is Dewayne Lucas, Karma's dad. Dewayne, this is Edna Garrett, the governor's wife," Kat introduced me to the woman who had my daughter shot. I blamed her unfairly.

The woman gave me a motherly hug and held me for longer than a stranger should, repeatedly thanking me as she did.

"You've raised an angel. She is literally an angel. I was so scared when that man had his gun pointed at my face. I've never been so afraid in my life, and your daughter, Karma, stepped in without a second thought for her own well-being. She stepped in between me and the gun, fought the guy, got shot, and still asked if I was ok as they took her in the ambulance. I cannot say it enough. You, sir, have raised a beautiful soul. You should be so proud... Hell, I know you are. I don't know how to repay both of you, but anything you need... Anything at all. I'll be right over there," she pointed to a waiting area, "I'm not leaving until she's released. I'll be right there! Thank you, Detective."

I stood there listening to a stranger bestow compliments on me that I didn't deserve.

"My husband wants to meet you both. My assistants are already preparing a ceremony at the governor's mansion where she'll get a medal of valor, and you'll both be the guests of honor." Then, she turned her attention to Kat. "Miss, be a dear, give him my number and get me a bottle of semi-cold water. I'm parched."

"Yassa, ma'am. Anything else I could do for ya, boss? You sho is lookin fine today, ma'am. Sho is!" Kat danced a little jig as she spoke, imitating a minstrel show.

I smiled, finally, then went back into the room, nodding a thank you to my friend, who walked away to give us time to talk.

I quietly looked around at all the flowers. I peeked through some of the gift bags, then picked up a stack of Hallmark cards and sat down to read them. I read one after the next, all of them were the standard, 'thank you for being you,' type cards, signed by an assortment of people. I set them all neatly back on the table and stood, staring down at her, listening to her breathe as she slept perfectly.

"What's this?" I said to myself, noticing something sticking out from under her pillow. It was another card. I pulled it out carefully.

Wonder Woman, in all of her glory, was pictured proudly on its cover. I opened it to read a handwritten message.

'Carol. I'm so proud of you! Get better soon! Love always, your sister from another mister, Diana Prince.'

Fuck!

Chapter 15: There's another part to this

Karma was awake for the brainstorming session about how to catch Charles. She said she felt fine and wanted to go with us when it was time, which was soundly rejected by me and Captain Thomson. It was two against one. Lieutenant Dan knocked and was welcomed into the room, which made it three against one.

I wondered why he was there, but during the course of normal conversation, he'd said that he met a woman the last time he was here, and was visiting her when he'd heard about Karma on TV. We included him in our relatively simple plans.

All we needed was the info from the security cameras, then we'd track down the Cybertruck and bust them both. Easy, peasy, lemon squeezy, as Karma put it. And I already knew Dan just wanted in so he could take all the credit. I was ok with that, none of that stuff meant anything to me.

We talked about the Wonder Woman card, and Karma explained its significance to everyone. It proved that Patricia had been in her room, and Karma was all too happy to let us all know that nothing bad had happened to her. Patricia wasn't the one we needed to worry about.

It was a moot point. They were both going down.

I still hadn't charged my phone or gone to the gas station yet, so I excused myself, letting everyone know I'd be back shortly.

"Hold on, I'll walk out with you," Lieutenant Dan said, jogging to catch up with me. "I've got a few quick errands to run myself. Me and my lady friend had dinner plans. Let me go get her settled and I'll come right back, then we'll go get that motherfucker."

When we went our separate ways, him to his triangle truck, and me towards my car, I turned around and went back to him.

"Hey, Dan, wait a minute." I must've been caught up in my feelings because as I reached out for a handshake, I embraced him in a hug instead. I thanked him for stopping by to check in on Karma, and I told him how much I appreciated him for always looking out for me back in our own district. I also apologized for being kind of an asshole in dealing with all of this, explaining that when it came to my daughter, I reacted to things differently.

He accepted it all graciously, and I ended my little heart-to-heart with a joke about meeting up for dinner at Bubba Gump's Shrimp Factory later in the week.

"As long as you're paying," he said with a laugh and a wave.

I walked back to my vehicle in high spirits. Today was going to be a good day.

"My phone seems like it doesn't want to hold a charge anymore. It's ok when it's plugged in, but as soon as I take it off, I get about 10 minutes, then it starts chirping at me with a low battery signal. What the hell is wrong with your city's electricity?" I asked both women in Karma's room.

"Wait, what? How the hell is my city at fault for your shitty phone battery?" Kat Thomson replied angrily.

"It's the infrastructure. Your backwoods, soup can and shoestring electrical lines haven't been updated since before she was born!" I pointed at a smiling Karma, who was lying in her hospital bed, reading through all of her thank-you cards. "Y'all are not technologically capable of dealing with the modern scientific advancements such as this iPhone. And why are you taking it so personal? Don't act like you didn't know this. That's why you carry that Android. You are basically carrying a messenger pigeon. A messenger pigeon that takes sub-par pictures."

I shook my head like I was disappointed. "You would never make it in my world, Kitty Kat. But I'm glad you found your place. Ain't we, sweet girl? We're happy for her, right?"

I moved over to Karma's bedside and put my hand on her shoulder because Captain Thomson had jumped out of her seat and was stepping towards me, ready to fight. She stopped when I bent down to kiss my daughter's forehead. I looked up at Kat and smiled. "Yes, ma'am?" I asked condescendingly, "Did you need something?"

"Fuck you, Dewayne. You little shithole face. You ain't no fancy, technical ass, scientist… you damn cock junkie. You little… dumbface… dickbird! I don't need no dog crap, iPhone-shit phone. Matter of fact, watch this, face boy!" A verbally flustered Captain Thomson grabbed my charger out of the wall socket, threw it on the ground, then stomped on it, smashing it into a thousand pieces, cussing as she did.

Karma and I nearly died laughing. It was the perfect comic relief to what was sure to be a very dramatic next day or two.

"You guys ok in here? I thought I heard something fall." Nurse Becky stuck her head in the door.

"No. Do you guys have any medicine for grown-up cry babies who can't take a joke? She's like a giant bull in a china shop. She destroyed my charger," I joked.

The nurse laughed and started to close the door.

"Wait, ma'am?" Kat called out. "My tiny friend here wanted to know if you had any single friends. He likes tall, clean-shaven men with muscles. He likes to be tossed around and manhandled. He's what they call 'a spinner'. He was too shy to ask for himself."

The nurse looked at me and asked, "Does race matter?"

"Nope. He likes all colors of the rainbow. They call him Skittles back home. Ain't that right?" Kat patted my knee.

"Oooh. Burn! Dad, she got you. Ha ha ha!" Karma laughed.

Nurse Becky laughed too and closed the door, but not before she told us that they sell chargers downstairs at the gift shop, but they close soon, so hurry up.

No one's heard from him yet?" I asked, looking at both Karma and Captain Thomson. Lieutenant Dan still hadn't come back to the hospital, and it had been over 4 hours since we'd last talked. We were also still impatiently waiting for the info about the license plates. I kept telling Kat to call her office for an update, but she assured me that they would call when they had something for us. It was an excruciatingly slow process.

"Let's just go, I'm ready to go home. Can you guys sign me out? I hate it here," Karma complained.

"No!" I didn't offer an explanation. I said what I meant, and there wouldn't be any more discussion about it.

We sat around for another half hour before I'd had enough. I told Kat to give me the number so I could just call myself.

"Damnit, Dewayne! Fine! I'll call. Gimme a minute, I'll be right back!"

She got up and walked into the hallway, as Karma and I talked about what she would wear to the Governor's ball.

"Ok!" Kat came through the door. "The good news is, I have some information. First, they traced the Cybertrucks' movements, and it was here, but only for about 2 minutes, then it drove to an address that I have right here. And it's not registered to either of them, by the way. Next, the hospital's footage does show that Patricia was here for about 45 minutes, and she left in a different vehicle. She was wearing nurses' scrubs when she left, so that's how she managed to get in and out without being noticed. They got the plates of the car she got into. It was an Uber. She was dropped off at a different location than where the truck went."

"OK, good!" I jumped up, ready to get started. "I'll go get him, you go get her. When the lieutenant comes back, Karma, tell him what we got going on. I'll turn on the Trace My Phone app. Send him to my location."

"Wait, there's another part to this," Captain Thomson said. "They've had this info for a while. The reason they didn't call me is because they'd already given it to Dan. He talked to them hours ago. He said he was with us. I think he went alone. I think someone wants to be the hero."

Captain Kat Thomson rode with me to the real-time location of the truck that Charles was driving. It was at the back of a large junkyard in an otherwise barren field. The yard had a huge maze of old, rusted vehicles, and when we pulled around the corner, we saw two Cybertrucks, one on top of the other. The one on the bottom was crushed by it's enormous weight.

"Goddamnit, Dan," I said under my breath, as we walked up to investigate. We had our guns out, but I knew we didn't need to.

There were several bullet holes alongside the body of the crushed vehicle, disproving the myth that they are bulletproof, and the driver's side window, as well as the windshield, were both shattered.

If this were the movies, I'd walk up, say a quiet prayer, then close my friends' still wide-open eyes, but Lieutenant Dan didn't have a face anymore. He'd been shot from the back of his head. The bullet opened a giant gaping hole where his face used to be. The part of his head that remained had been pressed down unnaturally because of the way that the roof had caved in. Both hands were handcuffed to the steering wheel, and large pieces of wood that looked like broken pallet planks were stabbed into different parts of his body. He looked like a life-sized pin cushion.

I took a deep breath, shook my head, and then walked back to my car. As I waited for Kat to call it in, I thought about the last conversation I'd had with the man, glad that I had the opportunity to thank him. He was a good guy.

I drove away, leaving Kat yelling at me to stop. I didn't, though, she was safer where she was. My gut told me that Patricia's Uber took her home to where she and Charles lived, so that's where I was headed.

Chapter 16: Click clack

I pulled into a quiet, nondescript, middle-class neighborhood. I imagined cookouts where the men stood around talking about what type of lawn feed they used on their grass, while the women gossiped about who hadn't yet adopted a gluten-free diet for their families.

I drove past 5938 Skillman Street at a normal speed just to get a look at the lot. It was a clean looking, two or three bedroom, rambler-style home, with an attached one-car garage, and a chain link fenced yard. The only difference between it and any of the other homes near it was the numbers on the mailbox that hung next to the front door. I parked down the road, close enough to see anyone coming or going, but far enough away that it didn't look like I was there for that house. I opened my laptop to make it look like I'd stopped to do some work.

I did a mental exercise that I learned in therapy, where I was to slow my breathing, then intentionally think about what I was feeling at that exact moment. It was a conscious meditation. I allowed myself time to reflect on my life. The highs and the lows. The good and the bad. I looked in the mirror and saw the reflection of a man who's lived a good life. I made a terrible mistake with how I've handled being a parent, but hopefully, when I'm being judged by the ultimate judge, my time on earth doing right will balance out the wrong. I can honestly say that I did my part to make the world a better place. I was part of the solution. I am the good guy.

I put my hand on my pistol. I didn't need to check if it was ready to fire or if the magazines were loaded. I knew they were, as they always are.

I took another slow, measured breath and accepted the peace I felt. I was ready to die. One way or another, this ends tonight, I thought.

Beep Beep Beep!

I was snapped out of my unnecessarily dramatic moment by a text from Captain Thomson, calling me a motherfucker for leaving her in a 'fucking deserted, rat infested, Mad Max looking wasteland', and how she was going to 'kick me right in my little Vienna sausage sized dick' as soon as she saw me next. 'On site, you half size butt face!'

I laughed, thankful for my friend. I sent back a response saying that she sounded hangry and that she needed a Snickers bar.

I sent a quick text to Karma, telling her I'd be on my way back to the hospital shortly (one way or the other), and right as I pressed send, the garage door at the Brown's house started to go up. A car with the Lyft symbol in the window pulled up to the curb, and I saw Charles get out, then quickly run inside.

I made my move. I ran to the house and managed to sneak under the door before it shut.

I crept inside and listened. The man was moving quickly in a different part of the house, as I could hear what I thought to be Charles emptying his closets and dresser drawers. It sounded like he was packing his suitcases. I had my gun out, moving slowly towards him, creeping silently down the hallway. I could hear him mumbling to himself almost happily, "Come on, Peppermints. Hurry up, Patty".

Then he stopped. I did too. Everything went silent. I heard the unmistakable 'click clack' of a gun being cocked, then nothing. I moved into a bedroom and hid behind a dresser. My ears strained to hear anything. He didn't call out. He made no sound, but I could sense him moving about the house, searching. It was so quiet, I felt like I was hallucinating. I'd lost my sense of direction. I couldn't tell if he'd passed me to the left or was standing just beyond the doorway to my right. We stood in absolute silence for what seemed like an eternity. It felt like he was standing in the doorway, just waiting. I'd begun to 'tell tale heart' the situation in my brain. I just knew he could hear my thoughts as the stillness running through my mind threatened to drive me insane.

Then, I heard him move. It was as if his paranoia had been satisfied, and he was ok to return to packing up his things.

Beep Beep Beep! Damn phone. I forgot to shut off my ringer.

Charles stormed into the room.

POP! POP!

I shot twice. Once in each of his biceps, causing him to drop his weapon.

I ran towards him and landed a well placed punch in his solar plexus, knocking him backwards against the wall, falling, and struggling for breath.

I stomped on his chest repeatedly, cussing angrily with each step. The man offered no resistance, the fight was over as soon as the gunshots rendered his arms useless.

I stopped, out of breath, and told him to get up.

"Dewayne, wait! Why are you doing this?" he asked.

"Get the fuck up, Charles. Now!"

"I can't…"

"YOUR FUCKING LEGS AREN'T HURT! GET THE FUCK UP! NOW! MOVE," I yelled.

POP! I shot a round into the floor next to his head.

Tired of waiting, I dragged him into the kitchen and propped him up against the lower cabinets, then handcuffed his right hand to the oven, his left to the refrigerator door, so he was spread out, with arms wide open.

I'd lost control. It was like I was seeing myself in the 3rd person, as I kicked and punched him relentlessly. When my fists tired, I hit him with kitchen items. I pummeled the man with everything that wasn't nailed down. A rolling pin, mason jars, a frying pan off the stove... Everything but the kitchen sink (if you'll pardon the pun).

He didn't yell or scream out in pain. Not once. He looked like he'd accepted his fate. Like he knew he deserved this punishment.

I slipped in his blood and fell, hitting my head on the counter as I did. I must've knocked myself out, because when I woke up, I was sitting in a chair, and Karma was standing next to me, patting my head with a cold rag.

"What the hell..." I looked around, shocked. "What are you doing here? Why are you here?" I demanded angrily.

"I came to help."

"I TOLD YOU TO STAY AT THE GODDAMN HOSPITAL, KARMA! DIDN'T I TELL YOU TO STAY AT THE FUCKING HOSPITAL? WHY ARE YOU HERE?" I was livid.

"You didn't respond to my texts. I thought you were..."

"GODDAMN IT! YOU'RE JUST LIKE…" I'd almost said, 'your mother', but the look on her face said it all. She got the point; she'd had enough.

"I'm sorry, sweet girl, I'm sorry. But hey, can you do me a favor? Can you go get my car for me? It's right down the street. Can you bring it down here, please?" I asked gently.

She nodded and asked if we were taking him to jail. I said yes, and promised myself that it would be the last lie I ever told her.

"She's a good girl, Dewayne. I'm glad I didn't kill her," Charles said.

I spit in his face, "Fuck you!"

He flinched.

"Why are you doing this, Dewayne? I thought we were friends."

"You thought we were friends? Is this how friends act in your world?" I asked, incredulous.

"Well, yeah. I mean, I already forgave you for betraying me… I thought that was water under the bridge. I thought we'd moved past that," he said sincerely.

"I betrayed you?" I couldn't believe what he was saying.

"Yes. When you did that background check on me all those years ago, because you didn't trust me. You had my knife analyzed, remember? I wouldn't have ever done that to you. Not as a friend."

"Charles, you murdered my fucking wife!"

"Yeah, but that was after. Plus, you didn't even like her. She sure as hell didn't like you. I did you a favor, pal." He actually believed what he was saying.

"YOU DECAPITATED MY BROTHER!" I yelled.

"Really? You're gonna hold that against me? I didn't even know you back then! You can't take that personal! I didn't even know you existed back then! Are you seriously trying to put that on me? You got to be one heck of a darn narcissist to think that I killed him to hurt you! You need help, man. That's not a normal way to think. T-Bone was a bad…"

"ENOUGH!" I jumped out of my chair and punched him in the face, over and over again. He just took it all. Never made a sound.

"It's not my fault, Dewayne," he finally said. "I can't help doing what I do. No more than you can help yourself from stopping to help a woman with a flat tire. It's who we are. You think hitting me is gonna change that? You think I don't beat myself up enough about it?" He spat out a tooth.

"I'm your real friend. I killed Dan for you. He was trying to get me to go after your daughter."

"SHUT UP!" I hit him again.

"I've known Dan Nash for years. He was one sick puppy. He's known where I've been the whole time. He's known what I've been doing. He could've busted me a long time ago. But did he? No. He loved hearing all the details about everything I did. He couldn't wait to talk about it. He also liked all the fame and the attention he got when he'd find the victims. Like he was some great detective or something. How do you think he was always first on the scene? That son of a gun. He framed a lot of bad people with my kills. The same way you did with your friend, Jhonny. Remember that? Dan wanted me to go after your daughter. He said she was getting too close. I did him for you, Dewayne. I'm a real friend, and this is how you repay me? By hitting me?"

"Hey, Dad?"

I looked up and saw Karma, then saw Patricia Brown directly behind her with a pistol pressed against my daughter's head.

"Um, dad… She wants you to let him go."

I pushed my gun into the side of Charles' bloodied head, "No!"

"She said she would kill me if you didn't," Karma said, carefully.

Charles spoke to his wife. "Babe, I packed. We're ready to go." He sounded tired. "I already have the perfect spot picked out, in Hennepin County. You'll love it there."

"Dad?" Karma sounded nervous.

I looked from Charles to his wife, to my daughter, and thought about all of the innocent lives torn apart by this one person. This monster.

He spoke again. "Babe, go get our stuff, let's go. Your friend can come too, it's ok, I know you missed her, but let's go. I'm ready to go."

"Un cuff him," Patricia said, "Now! Or she dies." She spoke calmly at first, then yelled, "NOW!" and hit Karma on the head with her pistol as unviolently as she could.

I pressed my gun into Charles' right eye, finger curled around the trigger.

"Dad, please…" Karma begged.

"Do you believe in God, little girl? I don't, I believe in people. And one thing I know about people is that they don't change. You are what you were made to be. Your dad's not a killer, he's the good guy. Ain't that right, Detective?" Charles spoke in his condescending tone.

"LET HIM GO! NOW!" Patricia yelled.

"There you go, baby, tell him. I love you so much." He smiled, even as blood flowed freely down his face.

"You don't get to feel love, motherfucker! Fuck you!"

He flinched.

POP!

I pulled the trigger. His head exploded.

Patricia, who stood still, stared at her husband's headless body for a second, then put her gun down and walked into the backroom. She returned with a suitcase, then gave Karma a long hug and a loving kiss on the cheek.

I stood and took an aggressive step towards them with my gun up, ready, but a look from my daughter froze me in my tracks.

The two women stood face to face, hand in hand, and had their final conversation without words. Patricia stepped back with tears in her eyes, took a final look at Charles, then walked away with her head down. We followed her outside and watched as she climbed into her car. Peppermint Patty waved, mouthed the words 'love you' to her friend, then drove off.

Karma turned and cried into my chest.

(When asked later about why I didn't let Charles go when Patricia held my daughter hostage, I answered that I knew she was never in danger. The gun was fake. I could see the orange plastic tip as soon as they walked in.)

I heard sirens coming our way. I squeezed my daughter's hand and told her I'd see her later at her apartment. She had a long night ahead of her.

"Ok," she said, then sadly turned and walked back into the house.

Chapter 17: Cashing in the governor's favor

The governor's ceremony wasn't as boring as I thought it'd be, but it was still just a bunch of politicians patting themselves on the back for being tough on crime, and sucking up to special interest groups for more money.

We sat at the same table with the Governor's family. I was seated directly across from their oldest son, who just happened to be the same guy I beat up for assaulting a woman in that office building. The one I went to jail for. He did his best to avoid the eye contact I insisted we have.

Karma was awarded a medal, and I had my proud dad moment as I walked her on stage, then stood back and watched her outshine all the chandeliers in the room.

She thanked me and Captain Thomson as her ultimate inspirations, then dedicated the award to her mom. Right before she walked off, she threw a handful of peppermints into the crowd, saying that those were for her sisters from other misters, Patricia and Celeste.

In the weeks that followed, I moved out to Karma's little backwoods city. It just made sense to me. She was there, Captain Thompson was there, and her husband, Billy Ro, my old best friend, became my new fishing buddy. I even started dating Nurse Becky (with the good hair).

There were no mourners at Lieutenant Dan's funeral. Nobody from the law enforcement community went. After Karma reported about all the things he did, his existence was basically erased, remembered only by anecdotes on what not to do. There was no officer's send-off, and no 21-gun salute. They didn't even give him a headstone.

My daughter became an even bigger star than she was before. She was in talks to have a book written about her life, with a movie to follow that.

My career was pretty much done. I just didn't have it in me anymore. I was in a good space. I enjoyed waking up happy every day. I'd done enough good in my life to where I could finally sleep peacefully, with a clear conscience, knowing I'd done my part.

It was a hard decision to actually retire, but when I did, I did it amongst my small group of friends and family, who were one and the same.

"What are you doing here?" Captain Thomson asked as I walked through the courthouse towards the jail.

"What are you doing here?" I asked back.

"I'm doing my job. You wouldn't know anything about that, though, would you, old man?"

"Ha ha, I guess not," I laughed as I kept walking.

"What's going on, Dewayne? Really, is everything ok?" She jogged to catch up to me just as the guard checked my credentials and allowed me passage through the metal detectors, to the holding cells.

"Yes," I called back to her, "I'm just cashing in the governor's favor. I'm good, I'll be right back!"

I sat in a legal call room and waited patiently as the guy who shot Karma during the attempted carjacking was brought in.

"Wait, you're not my lawyer," the man said as the officer left and closed the door behind him. "GUARD, WAIT! THIS IS NOT MY LAWYER! THIS IS NOT MY FUCKING LAWYER! GUARD!"

THE END